elephants in the bush

and other Yamatji Yarns

elephants in the bush

and other Yamatji Yarns

CLARRIE CAMERON

Magabala Books

First published 2013, reprinted 2018, 2019
Magabala Books Aboriginal Corporation, Broome, Western Australia
Website: www.magabala.com Email: sales@magabala.com

Magabala Books receives financial assistance from the Commonwealth
Government through the Australia Council, its arts advisory body. The State
of Western Australia has made an investment in this project through the
Department of Culture and the Arts in association with Lotterywest.

Designed by Mark Thacker, Big Cat Design
Printed and bound in Australia by Griffin Press

9781922142146 (paperback)
National Library of Australia Cataloguing-in-Publication entry
Cameron, Clarrie.
Elephants in the bush and other Yamatji yarns/Clarrie Cameron.
Aboriginal Australians-Western Australia-North-West-Social
life and customs.
Short stories, Australian.
A823.4

Australian Government

Australia Council
for the Arts

Government of Western Australia
Department of Culture and the Arts

lotterywest
supported

I dedicate this collection of yarns to my father,
Leedham Cameron Snr, and to my Uncle George
Curley. Both of them were exceptional storytellers.
When I was small us kids would sit with our mouths
open drinking up their stories.

One particular yarn was about when they got a job
horse breaking. It was Leedham's turn to ride the
fresh-broken horse and it would not stop bucking.
When it was lunchtime the horse was still bucking
and showed no sign of stopping. Leedham was getting
hungry so George had to sit on the top rail with a ging
(slingshot). As the horse bucked past him he shouted,
'Open yer mouth.' Leedham opened his mouth and
George shot a piece of rolled up damper into it.

This story is true because Dad and Uncle George
said it was.

CONTENTS

Introduction and Acknowledgements

When I was a little tacker, in the 1940s, we were a poor group of Aboriginal families who lived in makeshift shacks and humpies in and around the backblocks of Cue and Meekatharra. We were real fringe dwellers. We had no TV, radio or DVD player. Us kids made our toys from bits and pieces we scrounged from rubbish dumps. We made our bikes and billycarts from parts we found around scrapyards. We had no electricity for lights so we sat around the open campfire and listen to each other yarning.

Our Elders were good at telling interesting and entertaining stories, spiced with humour to keep the attention of even the most restless youngsters. The storytellers were important to our community, they kept us sane and relieved the everyday tension of living in an oppressive society. The government, local police and, in many cases, rough station bosses, put a strain on Aboriginal people. But in the evenings, around the campfire, all was forgotten. These stories taught us to laugh at hard times and to smile at whatever the world threw at us.

No person exists alone. For me to say that this is my book would not be correct in any way. These stories are not just mine alone — they belong to all of us. I may have written them but they belong to the many who lived them.

I must thank my brother, Bobby Cameron (Cowboy), my cousin, Keith Narrier (Beasly) and my nephew, Francis Callow (Big Alf). When we were sitting around the fire and telling yarns, these three always ended up saying that someone should write these stories down.

Cowboy and Beasley have both said that if they were not written down before we were dead they would be lost forever. Many of the people have passed on. If the ones who have died read them from wherever they may be, they will be able to say, 'That was me in that yarn, I was there and I did that.' Sometimes when I tell a yarn I have to pull up and rest and sometimes shed a quiet tear for those who were with me then and have passed on forever.

For those people who have encouraged me, held my hand, patted me on the back, given me a comforting hug and assisted me to get these stories finished and printed I say a heartfelt, 'Thank You.'

In no particular order I say a big thanks to: Leonie Boddington, Doreen Mackman, Godfrey Simpson, Charmaine Green, Paige Finci, Amy Cargill, Leila Jabour, Tracy Green, Chrystieanne Woollett, Regina Gloede and my two sons, Trevor Martin and Duncan Cameron, who have watched my back all the way.

I am grateful to David Ronan who offered to read the first draft. When I saw him laughing and smiling for over two hours I knew I had accomplished my purpose. I also give special thanks to Yamaji Aboriginal Languages Corporation, Yamatji Marlpa Aboriginal Corporation, Bundiyarra Aboriginal Community Corporation and Irra Wangga Language Centre for very real and moral support.

Many thanks to all those folk who are not mentioned here who have been and still are part of these stories.

Clarrie Cameron

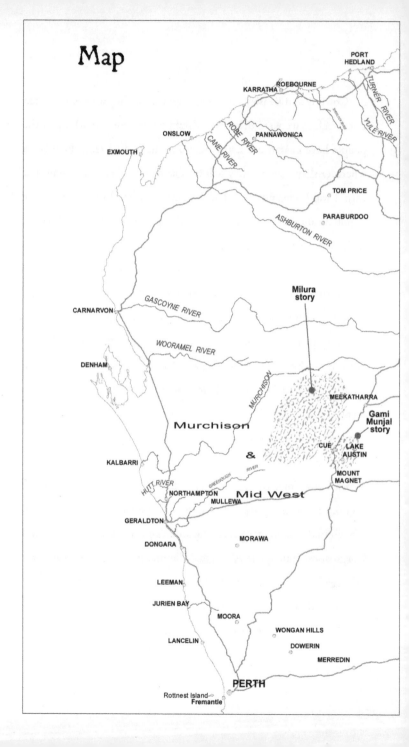

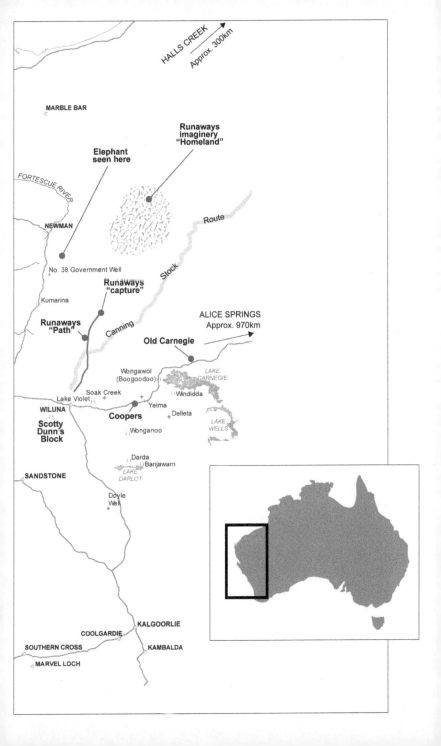

Milyura (snake) on the Loose

I was just a little kid then. I must have been about eight years old. My father worked on this station because it was right in the middle of our tribal country. My grandfather came from here and his people before him, came from all around this country. This was our country, this was our homeland.

Our family was made up of Grandmother, Ngaba, and Grandfather, Gami. My mother was Gracie and my dad was Donny. Then there was us kids. Me and my brother Blooch. My proper name was Kitchener, everyone called me Kitch except the old Winja Boss because he was the one that named me. Winja Boss always called me Kitchener. My young brother's proper name was Blucher, but everyone just called him Blooch. Everyone except the Winja Boss that is, because it turned out that he'd also given him his name. Must have been named after those two blokes the Winja Boss always talked about, a couple of ringers he used to work with. They must have come from that other station Old Boss always called 'Overseas'.

Long before I was born Winja Boss left the station when his father was still alive and went to that place called Overseas. It must have been a real big run too because it had a lot of stock on it — and thousands and thousands of turkeys. Old Boss spent a lot of time just shooting turkeys on that run.

He was a single man then. His proper name is Patrick Donovan but we all just called him Winja, or old, Boss. His son Robert runs the place now and we call him Young Boss. He thinks he's a big man but he never answers back when Winja Boss growls at him.

Sometimes Winja Boss hides a bottle of whisky up in the woolshed and then he takes Gami Tommy with him to talk 'man's talk'. My brother and me sometimes sit a little bit away from them listening to them talking 'man's talk'. When Winja Boss has a few drinks he always tells my Gami stories about shooting turkeys. Must be that, with some whitefellas, shooting turkeys was real 'man's business'. When Gami drinks some of the whisky and listens to Winja Boss he always shakes his head and nods his head. Winja Boss reckons that he spent all his time, on that other station called Overseas, just shooting turkeys. Must have been a funny bloody place because he never talks about the sheep or what sort of cattle they had, only those bloody turkeys.

When it gets cold Winja Boss's hip gets so crook that he can't walk properly and he tells Gami about the time one of those turkeys shot him there and nearly crippled him. When I grow big I am going to buy a horse and go to that property called Overseas and see for myself just how big those turkeys are — if they can shoot back they must be bloody queer turkeys. I'll buy a good shotgun just in case one of the buggers attacks me.

When Winja Boss gets real excited he tells Gami about one particular paddock on that Overseas station where the turkeys were real savage and a lot of Australian turkey shooters got killed. They must have been good ringers too because Winja Boss calls them all his 'good mates'. He sometimes mentions that one special paddock but I can't remember the name just now. If I go that way I'll have to remember to keep right away from that paddock.

Winja Boss reckons it was sad that he couldn't take Gami with him that time. He said the government Native Affairs said Gami was not allowed to leave the station because he was full of blood. I couldn't work that one out because I thought the more blood a person had the better chance he would have of staying alive if one of those turkeys shot him. Not only that but I always thought everybody was full of blood.

When Winja Boss got shot they brought him home on a big ship and that was where he met Old Missus. She was a nurse and looked after him real good so he brought her back to the homestead and married her.

Winja Boss reckons, never mind that she's a Pom, she's still a bloody good nurse and very handy to have on the station. Sometimes if us kids get sick she gives us some castor oil or cough medicine and fixes us up. Sometimes she rubs our chests with Vicks. Grandmother rubs it off and puts emu oil on instead.

Old Missus is a good nurse and Gami reckons she's better than a doctor. Gami reckons she was a real pretty one when Old Boss brought her home. He reckons she was a real flash nyarlu too. Old Missus lets me and Blooch feed all the chooky-chookies, ducks and geese and all the work dogs. We both look after the new puppies too because when they get big they'll be good work dogs. Old Missus reckons when I get big enough to muster sheep I can have one of the pups for my own work dog. I already picked out my pup. I picked a little red cloud up by the tail and hung him upside down. He didn't even whinge or cry so I know he'll be a good sheepdog when he gets big. I picked him up by the tail every time we fed his mother and he never gave one squeak. He just looks at me with his tongue hanging out like he's smiling at me. He already likes me I think. The roof of his mouth is black too, which means he will be one of the best sheepdogs around. A lot people don't know this and I don't know why it means this, it just does.

Gami is too old to ride after sheep any more so he stays home around the homestead and looks after the garden and chops the wood for the cook. When he finishes chopping wood the cook gives him a big piece of brownie and a mug of tea with plenty of sugar. Me and Blooch work too and Old Missus gives us lollies for our good work, sometimes liquorice or dried apricot.

Gami used to be a good ringer once and a rodeo champion bucky-jumpy too. Old boss reckons Gami was the best at tail-throwing a bull too. Tail-throwing is when you grab a bull by the tail and throw him onto the ground. Winja Boss reckons he rode right behind Gami and castrated the mickey bull — male calf — before he hit the ground. They both old now and Winja Boss got that crook hip and Gami got too much rheumatic. He got one stiff mambu, knee, too. They both cripple properly now, both winja.

ONE DAY OLD GAMI finished all the wood cutting and finished his brownie and tea, and he laid down under that big giji tree to have a sleep. Ngaba had taken her bit of brownie and went up to her camp to have a rest from the heat. Me and Blooch had some mintie lollies and two dried pears that the cook gave us for feeding all the chooky-chookies and crept close to Gami to finish off a bit of tea that was left in his pannikin. We sat very quiet a little bit away from Gami because we were not allowed to make noise when he was having his 'dinner goon-goon'. We were not allowed to make any noise but Gami could snore so loud he could wake himself up. To save us getting the blame if he did wake up we shifted to another tree a good bit away so we could play 'drovers' draughts' using different coloured sheepshit, or gurna for taws.

In hot weather Gami only wore a waistcoat and dungaree trousers. He had an Akubra hat that must have been forty years old. It was torn in a few places and showed where sweat had come through.

Gami was snoring like a broken-winded horse but it was strong and regular, which was normal for him. All the work dogs were asleep in their kennels and the camp dogs were chained up under the trees. We couldn't let the kangaroo dogs off their chains when there were sheep in the next paddock. It was me and Blooch's job to feed the dogs and make sure they had plenty of water. There was no noise from the chooky-chooky yard because a chicken hawk had flown over the yard and they'd all rushed into the shed for cover. They wouldn't come out until the late afternoon cool wind came up.

Gami gave a very loud fart and an extra loud snore and rolled over onto his stomach with his arms level with his shoulders and his hands under his face. Me and Blooch were proud of our Gami because he could snore and fart louder than anybody else we knew. We both held our breath for a few minutes for fear of waking him. We quickly finished our game and lay back in the shade. Everything was quiet and still — not a thing was stirring for miles around.

I was just dozing off and starting to dream about when I would be big enough to go to that Overseas station where they had more turkeys than normal stock. I was thrashing my mind about the name of that paddock with the turkeys that could shoot back. I wouldn't get shot in the hip like Winja Boss did. I'd make sure I had a good twelve-gauge shotgun with me. The name of that paddock would come back to me yet.

Just when I was about to get a headrope on that name I heard Gami give a low groan. It was not a normal sort of snore or cough or anything, but a groan as if he was in bad pain. Because I was bigger than Blooch I knew I was responsible for looking after Gami. I thought of the stomach poison the last yardman had and all the noise he'd made before he died — but Gami made a groan more like the one the shearers' cook made after he'd drunk all the metho from the tilly lamp. I slowly opened one eye and looked lazily towards the old fella. One look and I sat straight up. Gami's eyes were looking straight at me and he was wide awake. Now, my Gami had very black skin and the whites of his eyes were showing so much that I couldn't see any other parts! That look they call 'terror'. I could see the sweat starting to show on his forehead even though he was in the shade — it started pouring out of him *and* he seemed to be shivering.

He said, 'Kitch, come here.'

I got up, wide awake now, and started to move quickly towards old Gami.

After my first step he said, in a low, carefully controlled voice, 'No, don't come too close, stand back a bit.'

'What, Gami, are you sick?' I asked.

'Don't come too close to me, milyura here,' he said, in a strangled, small voice.

By this time Blooch was awake and as he rubbed his eyes he looked around carefully and asked, 'Where?' He'd heard Gami say 'milyura' and Blooch was one very frightened bloke of snakes. He got up and moved towards Gami because, to Blooch, the safest place to be was as close to his Gami as he could get.

'Boy, don't you come close, snake here right next to me!' Gami told him.

Me and Blooch both had the wind up by this time. We were jumping up and down and lifting our feet very high and looking to make sure there was nothing under them. We still couldn't see any snake but we knew Gami's word was gospel truth. Blooch's eyes showed as much white as Gami's and he'd broken out in a sweat too. We asked Gami where this milyura was supposed to be.

'Under my ribs, next to my body,' he said. 'Don't come too close, go and get the boss.'

'Old or young one?' I asked.

'Any bloody one would do!' he hissed, 'but get them bloody quickly and make sure they don't come too close and disturb this milyura.' The exasperation really poured out of him now.

I stepped back to get a good look at the milyura next to his body. Blooch said he could see part of the milyura's tail from where he was standing and was slowly backing as far away from his favourite gami as he could get. So much for family loyalty and affection.

The milyura must have been living in the wood heap and after Gami finished cutting wood, when everything was quiet, the milyura must have come out and gone straight to the nearest shade. That was the very same shade Gami had chosen. Gami, laying sound asleep, offered a safe place for the milyura.

A few feet of the milyura was laying alongside the old man and the head was tucked under his left armpit. Blooch and I froze for a minute but the milyura saw us and tried to snuggle closer underneath Gami. The old man pushed his body closer to the ground trying to prevent it from getting underneath him. I could see the old man trembling like a young horse being broken in. From some tremendous store of willpower Gami controlled himself and did not move. I could see he was too frightened to breathe properly.

Blooch was getting ready to make a break for it. Suddenly he bolted like a young brumby coming out of a stockyard. He went towards the camp where Ngaba was napping, he went so fast he would've made a good candidate for the next Stawell Gift. Given the right sort of incentive I thought he showed evidence of being good Olympic material too. I watched him charge into the camp and, as he charged inside, he must have stepped on old Ngaba's guts because she gave an almighty bloodcurdling shout that could wake the very souls from hell. That shout must have been heard at the next station fifty miles away.

Her shout startled the kangaroo dogs and other camp dogs woke from their slumber and started an unholy uproar. This chorus was soon joined by the dogs in the kennels and was added to by all the chooky-chookies in the pen. They must have thought a mob of hawks was attacking them along with a couple of eaglehawks thrown in as well. By now everybody on the station must have been awake.

Mum jumped out from our tent next door to Ngaba's and nearly tore down the ridgepole as she tripped over a bucket and a loose tin dish. As she sidestepped a kerosene tin she stepped into the hot coals where she had been cooking — she sprang about ten feet in the air. I thought that Blooch must have got his athletic prowess from her side of the family because that leap sure had a lot of potential. Seemed like we had some sporting talent hidden in our family.

All this time I'd stood where I was, not too far away from where old Gami was pinned down by that milyura. Every person or animal that could make a noise was either shouting at the top of their voice or making some sort of effort to announce to the world that they had been very seriously disturbed. Every animal or person, that is, except for the two main actors in this story who were both staying very quiet. And I was still cemented to the ground.

The next thing I heard was a thunderous shout that came from the direction of the big house. It was Winja Boss. My heart was in my mouth — ever since I was a little tacker, I was taught to fear and respect that particular bellow. That voice was omnipotence personified and the ultimate authority over half a million acres of some of the finest station country in the state.

I broke from my frozen stand and ran towards Winja Boss. As I drew near I had to swallow hard to get the words out. I was not a stutterer but that day I did a good imitation. Somehow the words sorted themselves out and Winja Boss finally got the story. He rushed inside and brought out his big twelve-gauge. I led him towards where old Gami was. We both pulled up short of where Gami and the milyura were getting acquainted rather intimately. As a matter of fact the milyura seemed to be taking a liking to old Gami. By this time there was Mum, Ngaba, Blooch, Winja Boss, Old Missus and me — and all the dogs — raising hell and making a big hullabaloo. This made old Gami even more of a refuge to the milyura and it was as close as he could be to the old fella.

'Stay back so I can shoot this milyura!' Winja Boss told everybody.

When Gami heard this he nearly had a heart attack because there was no way to shoot the milyura without also shooting Gami. Winja Boss had the same thought and he started to panic a bit too. His jaw was so tight I expected him to bite through his pipe stem.

The milyura took a look around at the crowd and wriggled even closer under Gami's neck. It moved around to the other side of

Gami's throat and up near his face. By this time it was pushing out its tongue and flicking it around Gami's eyelashes and over his lids. Gami shut his eyes tighter. His legs were trembling like a leaf but his upper body was as still and rigid as stone. I could see the muscles in his face twitching. One muscle was moving so much I thought the milyura might take offence.

The milyura twisted around and put its nose under Gami's armpit and started flicking its tongue among the hairs under Gami's arm. I hoped Gami wasn't ticklish. The milyura was frantically trying to snuggle further beneath the old man and Gami pushed his guts further into the ground, as far as he could.

The milyura soon gave up trying to get underneath Gami and decided to go over the top of him. It came up the side of his body and over to where Gami's belt was — it looked to go down his trousers. Gami slowly pushed his guts out as far as he could so the milyura couldn't find a way down. When the milyura realised he couldn't escape that way he turned his head around — and saw a hole. There was a hollow place where Gami's waistcoat was pulled tight across his back. To everyone's horror, the milyura crawled in and curled up inside the space. He had found a safe place to hide and settled in.

Gami was really pinned down now. I could see where his toenail had made a hole in the ground where his leg had been shaking. Gami had a very long nail on that toe. His eyes were still wide open and there was a bit of white froth leaking from the corner of his mouth, like he had been eating poison or something. He gave a sort of half-hearted croak, like a frog with a sore throat.

I remembered that a milyura could sleep all through winter. That could mean Gami would have to stay where he was all that time. Us kids might have to bring him his feed and water. I'd have to do his work and cut the wood for the big house. I hoped he would find a way out from under that milyura soon because I hated cutting wood.

All this time the dogs kept up a constant chorus even though they'd forgotten why they started in the first place. Ngaba was shaking like a leaf and yowling and shaking her hands and sobbing just like Gami was already dead. Mum was trying to calm her down and the old missus was holding her hand. Blooch was standing like he was going to say something but nothing came out of his mouth. Winja Boss was looking to me as if I knew of some way to get this milyura out of my Gami's back. I think I just stood there with my mouth open. I couldn't think of anything to say either. Winja Boss told us all to stand back and for Blooch to do something about shutting the dogs up so that he could think properly. Blooch ran and began to throw water over the dogs to shut them up. When he ran out of water he started to throw sand over them so the last time I looked the dogs were covered in mud. They stopped their noise though. I would not have thought of the sand. Blooch was a thinking bloke it seems.

I finally found my voice and said, 'If we could cut the sides of Gami's waistcoat we could lift the top half off.' I didn't think it was an important suggestion but Winja Boss had heard me and told me to go and get the old shears from the shed. I was glad for something to do and ran to the shed and brought back the old shears we used for cleaning up maggoty sheep. Winja Boss very carefully cut along both sides of the waistcoat and lifted it off with a rake.

Well, that milyura got a surprise! He raised his head up in the air and slowly turned around to look at us all standing around staring. I suppose we all looked like enemies to him. He must have decided that the only friend he had was Gami because he tried to go down Gami's trousers again.

I had a rude thought just about then but decided it was not the right time or place so I kept quiet, although I may have had a silly grin on my face, which I wiped off quickly and made my face look serious before my mother saw me. She might think I was making fun of my Gami.

The milyura was becoming very baja by this time and was flicking his tongue along the side of Gami's ribs. Gami's toenail was digging quite a big hole in the ground now.

Finally the milyura saw a clear opening back towards the woodpile. That milyura took off towards that woodpile as fast as he could move. He must have thought he was going to escape but he never took account of Winja Boss — a man who had once shot a great many dangerous turkeys. When the milyura was far enough away from old Gami Winja Boss blew that milyura away with the twelve-gauge.

It was the very same shotgun I intended to take with me when I went to that station called Overseas. With that shotgun I might become famous for shooting those savage turkeys even though I still couldn't work out how a turkey could shoot back. I'll have to ask Blooch if he can remember the name of that paddock over there where the turkeys were real dangerous.

Winja Boss walked over to Gami and told him that the milyura was dead and it was safe for him to get up now. Well Gami gave a low groan that came from deep in his chest but he lay as still as he could. He reckoned he could still feel that milyura lying on his back. He said he could feel it poking its tongue around his ribs and along his face. He told Winja Boss he could still feel that slimy, slithering milyura trying to get into his trousers. Winja Boss told him to look up but he only opened one eye and asked if Old Boss was talking truefella. The old boss took his arm to lift him up but the old fella jumped about six yards away and gave a great yell.

He slowly looked down the left side of his body to see if that milyura was still there. He turned carefully to his right side and did the same. When Ngaba touched his arm and said it was all clear he leaped straight up in the air. He came down heavy on his weak leg, which collapsed beneath him. But didn't stay down for long. He sprang up on his two arms and one good leg twisting in the air like an acrobat and landing on the ground shaking like a new-broken horse. Once again he jumped up in the air looking down to his right side to see if that milyura was still there. As he came down he twisted like a rodeo horse and tripped backwards and tipped old Ngaba head-over cartwheel. She hit the ground and rolled over backwards. Ngaba had stopped crying and her eyes were sticking so far out that I could have knocked them off with a stick. She forgot all about Gami's predicament and scrambled towards the other side of the giji tree. The old man was much more dangerous than when he was being held down in a stranglehold by a rogue milyura.

Gami was still springing up in the air — up he went and down he came. Up he went and down he came. Up and down again. All the time swinging his eyes from left to right then back again. I was hoping he'd make up his mind whether to stay up or down.

Gami rushed towards Ngaba and the giji tree. I didn't know whether he wanted protection and comfort from her or whether he wanted to do her physical damage. Ngaba was also in two minds and got behind the tree. But Gami went straight up that giji tree, all the time looking around from side to side for that milyura.

Mum, who mostly took life's calamities with a calmness that only wives and mothers can possess, was screaming something awful — she was worried that Gami had done serious damage to Ngaba. She wasn't thinking of poor Gami. Ngaba was looking nervously at this crazy man of hers up the tree. She looked around her and spied a clear pathway to the camp. She jumped over the wheelbarrow, smartly sidestepped a heap of timber, barely missed a pole, then, like a jockey on the home stretch with the cup in sight, she was gone. Nice bit of speed too for an old girl, Blooch sure got his running ability from her side of the family. At the sight of Ngaba sprinting towards them, all the kangaroo dogs started to cheer her on at the very top of their voices. After all they were her dogs and they all enthusiastically applauded her valiant effort. A hell of a racket.

Blooch was standing back about twenty yards and didn't know who to fear most, Gami who was safe and alive or the milyura who was dead. I moved around to get a good look at Gami up the tree and listen to Winja Boss who was trying to get him to come down. Winja Boss even picked up the dead milyura to show him it was really dead but Gami shrieked and only climbed higher. He was shaking so much he nearly fell out.

Finally the branch he was on gave way under his weight and Gami hit the ground. He sprang upright and made a beeline for the camp. He sidestepped the same wheelbarrow but hit the timber that Ngaba had missed. When he hit the ground he gave a Rambo roll and was up and gone again. Now that was a runner if ever I saw one. Maybe Blooch got his athletic ability from Gami's side after all. The dogs saw him coming and cheered him on louder than they had done for Ngaba. This time it was old Gami's favourite sheepdogs who cheered the loudest. Ngaba saw him coming and stepped sideways like a rugby player to avoid him, very neatly done too.

Gami ran straight into his lean-to humpy and hid under the blankets. There he lay curled up like a dog, crying and shaking. Ngaba stood away from the humpy. I don't think she fully trusted her dearly beloved anymore.

The dogs finally ran out of breath or energy or both. They had been at it constantly for at least two hours, which was a good effort. Mum went up to the camp to tend to Ngaba and put the billy on the fire. Winja Boss tossed that milyura into the rubbish bin and took the empty cartridge out of the shotgun and put it away. The old missus told him she would go up to the camp and check on Ngaba. Seemed like everyone had forgotten that my Gami was the one who wrestled that giant milyura and, to my thinking, he should have got some attention and sympathy, so me and Blooch wandered up slowly towards the camp, which was settling down again. Winja Boss caught us up and said he would check on Gami. Us menfolks had to stick together so me and Blooch got into step with the winja boss.

When we got to the camp we all three looked across at the three women. They were all sobbing, even the old missus. Why the old missus was sobbing was beyond my thinking, because she had not come anywhere near the milyura. Us men looked at them with disdain and went in to see old Gami. Winja Boss felt Gami's hand and sent me to the woolshed to get some medicine. I knew what medicine he meant. He told me not to let the old missus see the bottle because she would run amok if she knew it was even on the station. Me and Blooch ran as fast as we could — we knew the hiding place for the whisky. Holding the bottle well down my shirt and with Blooch as a loyal escort we brought the magic elixir back to them. He gave a half full pannikin to Gami and got one for himself. He reckoned a man should not drink alone and, seeing he was Gami's oldest friend, it was proper for him to be by Gami's side in times of trouble. Us two boys sat close by and gave moral support. Our Gami's welfare was very dear to both of us. And Winja Boss had given us both our names so we were obligated to him as well.

After a few more drinks the pannikins were both empty and Gami was a lot calmer. Ngaba said she was going to sleep with Mum, and us two boys could sleep with Gami. It suited us and it suited Winja Boss and Gami too — they made short work of that bottle of whisky.

By this time Gami was well over the shakes and was talking about how he had single-handedly held that milyura down to protect us two boys. Winja Boss said what a brave man Gami was and went on to say that it was a pity he couldn't have taken Gami with him when he had gone to that Overseas place. Then he said goodnight to Gami and us boys. He said that when we grew up we would be brave blokes just like our Gami. I had my doubts about proving my bravery by wrestling some giant milyura but I would certainly go to that Overseas place and kill some of those turkeys.

As I was dozing off I dug Blooch in the ribs and asked him if he could remember the name of that Overseas paddock, that one Winja Boss always said had the very dangerous turkeys. Old Gami must have been listening because he gave a snort and a loud fart before he said, 'That paddock called Gilli Pilli, don't you remember, Winja Boss always talk about that Gilli Pilli every Anzac Day.'

Gami
Munjal

During the years before the Second World War the West Australian government had some very tough laws regarding the treatment of Aboriginal people. Gami Munjal was one of those who was sent away to Rottnest Island for some crime or other. He had escaped and swam from Rottnest to the mainland and walked home to Cue — more than four hundred miles. He followed the bush country and wore sheepskin on his feet so the black trackers couldn't follow him. He came into my father's camp just after sundown and Dad greeted him warmly and gave him a feed and some tea. Dad was a skin-nephew to the old fella.

They yarned well into the night and the old man told us the story of his escape. I was about five years old and my brother was about three. My brother and I were a couple of small black boys and we had a way of doing things our own special way. Maybe we were somewhat feral but we seemed to survive well enough. Mum had to teach us to keep our clothes on when she took us to town shopping. We were absorbed by the story Gami told us. Before us two small ones went to sleep, Gami Munjal had grown into our hero because he had defied the wicked whitefella system and had won.

In the following months Gami Munjal used to come into our camp from the direction of the bush and Dad would give him some tea, sugar and tobacco. Sometimes the old man brought some cooked guwiyarl, yalibirri or marloo meat, that's goanna, emu and kangaroo.

My brother and me looked forward to him coming in because he brought us a billy-can full of bardi grubs, bimba gum or thardunga seeds. We loved our old Gami. He was our hero.

THE POLICEMAN CAME TO our camp one day and asked Dad if he had seen a native named Tommy Peter. Dad said he had not seen the old man for a long time. He believed Tommy Peter was in prison down in Fremantle. The policeman said he had been sent to Rottnest Island and was missing, probably had escaped. 'Escaped?' all the other blackfellas said, 'we didn't think anyone could escape from Rottnest.' They all said that none of them had seen Tommy Peter for several years and agreed, in unison, 'he must be dead.' The policeman rode off on his pushbike and must have thought that we were a lot of morons. They sure acted like a dumb mob, especially around policemen.

One day old Gami came through the bush giving a long low whistle. There were only us two little fellas at home. Mum and Dad had gone specking for gold and left us littlies to look after the camp and water the dogs. We went to the bush and called to Gami that it was safe to come into camp and that Dad was away. We thanked Gami for the bimba he had brought us and waited patiently for Dad to come home. The afternoon dragged on and we two small boys became tired and bored and wanted something to do.

Mostly we thought of some mischief.

I looked towards the road to town and started staring hard. Gami Munjal was very short-sighted because he had suffered from 'sandy blight'. Gami asked what I had seen and I said that it looked like a policeman on his bike coming towards the camp.

'Ija Gami, mardanyu coming?' I said. 'Ija, mardanyu all right, look like plijiman.' Our Gami started to crawl backwards and slithered away from the camp. He whispered to us boys, 'Be very quiet and when the plijiman come say you never seen me.'

We promised him faithfully that we would never say anything to send him back to gaol and watched as he slowly got to his feet and, running at a stoop, took off for the bush. He put on a good spurt of speed and impressed us — we didn't know he could run so fast at his age. Us two brothers thought we never saw anything run like our Gami. He was our hero.

We never saw our Gami for a long time and when Dad asked if the old man had been around we both, very innocently, said we had not seen him.

'He might have taken off across Wiluna way or Sandstone country,' we said.

'That could be right,' Dad said, 'the old fella has people over that way who will look after him.'

'Yes,' we agreed, 'that might be where he is! We miss him though.'

We were naughty little fellas and I think we mostly missed the bimba and bardies. We agreed that we should not have frightened the old fella, but we never told Dad what we'd done.

Elephants in the Bush

T here were five of us living in South Hedland; the Faithful Five. We all liked a drop of that which cheers and had been drinking steadily, on and off, for the last two years. We all knew someone who had gone to a Dry Out centre and declared themselves to be an alcoholic. We'd not gotten that far yet. All of us were a bit above lowering ourselves to that stage. We were not alcoholics.

Grease rented a house from Homeswest. Butch was his star boarder. Uncle Cowboy and Grady turned up for a weekend's visit; that was three months ago. Every time my wife kicked me out I gravitated towards that house. I was a frequent visitor. There I found all the liquid sympathy and overproof understanding I so rightfully deserved. Wasn't I thoughtful enough to live with the woman? (Mind you the house was in her name and she received her own benefit cheque, but I fulfilled the role of man of the house, which meant that she should have been grateful.) At Grease's house I got considerable counselling from those who had been through married life, and from those whose wives had left them.

Each of them knew that a woman just didn't understand that a man needed liquid nourishment for the good of his health and for support of his very soul. Good wholesome counselling administered by older men (preferably ex-stockmen) and washed down with liberal amounts of moselle was just what the bush philosophers recommend.

I could not find a more qualified group of experts. We all drank a bit. But we were not alcoholics.

Grease had been married twice. No more needs to be said. Butch had been married once and had a few kangaroo jobs since then. So he was very knowledgeable when properly inspired by some good red from the Barossa Valley or, more so, a strong port from Upper Swan.

Uncle Cowboy was another story altogether. He had been married once and she'd left after twenty years of trying to reform him. He had had twice as many kangaroo jobs as Butch and there were a few joeys around to vouch for that.

Grady was more conservative. There had been a wife and somewhere there was a son. He owed nobody anything and as long as his dole came on time he was happy. He said a blackfella on the dole meant Bob Hawke was paying us mob rent after having dispossessed us in the first place.

As I said, I was living with a lady at the time and, in my sober moments, thought of getting a job and settling down permanently with her. It seems that every time I had a sober thought and good intentions, one of my mates got a dole cheque. This meant I had to go over to Grease's house to collect what was owed to me. Not just for the grog mind you. I wasn't an alcoholic.

It was just that someone there always seemed to owe me money. It was hot country and on a hot day it was only polite to offer a guest a cold beer. I'm the sort of person who would never insult a friend by refusing a drink. Quite often it would take three days to collect the ten dollars that was owed to me and by the time I got home I would owe some other person twenty dollars. Never mind, my cheque would be in the bank tomorrow. And what are friends for anyway?

It was just as well we were not alcoholics.

When I got home I always promised the missus that I would get a job. One of the Faithful knew of a guy who'd been a good grader driver once who knew a fella who might want a loader driver who might get a contract for some work that might be going out the back of some town somewhere ...

I promised the good lady of the house that when I got that job I'd save up for that trip to Perth I'd promised her two years ago. When that job came through I'd even buy her that dress she always looked at in K-mart. And the kitchen could do with some new curtains. I'd even pay the rent for a month or so. I drank a bit but I was not an alcoholic.

Some relation — I can't remember who now — had passed away and the funeral was to be held down in Meekatharra. It was only right that I go down for the funeral. I went over to Grease's place to see if the Faithful were going to the funeral. I knew Uncle Cowboy and Grady had that car that had been sitting in the front yard the last few weeks. They said it was a good goer, it was a four-man self-starter. It should get us there and back. When I got to the house Butch opened the door and I got a shock. Butch was all busted up with skin off his nose and a new bend in it. There were scratches all down his arms and across his chest. He looked as if he had come off second best to a big red boomer. It looked as if he'd tried his luck with the boomer's brother too. His shoulder and arm were bruised and he had difficulty opening the door for me. Well, I blew up at them others for bashing the poor harmless sod. I asked who had done the damage to the poor bugger and if they'd like to try their luck at doing the same thing to me. It was a shame because they were all tougher than he was and a lot bigger too. Butch was the type who wouldn't hurt a fly but was always being picked on — he was the littlest chicken in the yard.

Grease told me not to get my drawers in a knot because nobody had laid a finger on the silly bugger. He grinned at me in that smirky, lopsided way that said I was a slow learner.

It just turned out that it had been Butch's turn to take the rubbish bin out to the kerbside for the rubbish truck in the morning. It had taken him two hours to get the bin from the back of the house to the front kerb. They said he didn't look too bad considering it had been a heavy bin. It was just as well he was not an alcoholic or else he might have really hurt himself.

45

I got my dole cheque and we took off after we filled up with petrol and sufficient liquid sustenance to get us as far as the next liquor outlet in Newman.

We had been drinking all the way and were feeling nice and mellow. Each one of us had reached the stage where it was appropriate to express our thoughts and give voice to all of our collective wisdom and knowledge. It seemed only right to share it with Butch who had been constantly complaining about his aches and pains. Every one of us thought that straight whisky was what he needed most to fix him up. Not too much though — just enough for medicinal purposes — we didn't want him to become an alcoholic.

We began a long discourse on the problem that was getting a lot of our people down. We all agreed on the evils that could come from alcohol dependency and the effect it could have on any one person. We spoke of all the blokes we had seen trying to climb up brick walls. We mentioned several blokes who had shot themselves after downing enough Johnny Walker. Another bloke we knew had told us he had seen pink elephants. That sounded like a load of crap because we had all been pretty drunk but had never reached the pink-elephant stage. We agreed that the story had been made up by that Christian mob to make us believe that grog was evil and to show us that we were relegated to the category of sinners. We spoke of drunken leprechauns and wondered if a drunken wudaaji would act the same.

This was hairyman country and I asked if we should leave a bottle for the little fellas at the next gumbu or piss stop. They told me to stop talking like an idiot and think of pink elephants instead. I told them that I would stop drinking if I ever reached the pink-elephant stage but I was not an alcoholic yet.

The liquid fortification had begun to have a soothing effect on all of us and the conversation died down slowly as we each reached that stage of quiet solitude — the one that drunks reach within themselves, keeping their thoughts to themselves.

I was watching the country change from the Hamersley Tableland country into mulga country as we approached the Murchison-Gascoyne pastoral area.

I was beginning to doze a bit and glanced towards a mulga thicket about two hundred yards ahead. There had been quite a few cattle on the side of the road after we had left Capricorn Roadhouse and right now, as were passing Well 38, I was looking at a bloody big bull. His tail seemed a bit thick as it swung back and forth and I blinked my eyes for a better look. That looked like an elephant's trunk. Another blink and it was still an elephant's trunk. I screwed my eyes to clear my vision and shook my head to clear the cobwebs and when I opened my eyes it was still an elephant.

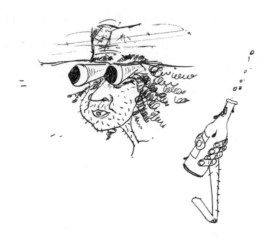

Not pink, thank goodness, but a dull grey. Nevertheless I must be going off. What was an elephant doing way out here? I must be seeing things.

I was in a worse state than I thought. Worse than the others. I waited for one of them to mention that they had seen an elephant in the bush. But no-one said anything.

Don't tell me I was in a worse state than Butch!

I was too afraid to say anything to the others because they might have committed me to the first hospital, police station or Dry Out place they came across. I was too young for that!

I must be an alcoholic.

What would my mother think?

What would that woman of mine think?

What would my kids think?

I always thought that one of them would go off first because they were older than I was and they drank more consistently than I did. Had I been deceiving myself all this time? Maybe that Christian mob weren't just blabbering a load of bulldust. Could there have been some truth in what they said?

That's it.

No more.

Full stop.

I'd had my last drink.

I would not be an alcoholic.

I was too young. I had a few more good years in me and I would make the most of them.

When this funeral is over I would go to church and give my heart to the Lord. No more drinking for me.

I had seen the light.

More than that, I had seen an elephant in the bush!

Kumarina was the next stop, just a few miles ahead. Kumarina is one of those joints that sits out beyond the outer edges of what we call the great outback. I would get out for a gumbu stop.

I'd have a feed and a free coffee for the driver.

I had not had a decent feed since the other day and sure needed something to get me back on my feet.

We pulled up in front of the roadhouse/pub and I turned to wake the others up but they were all wide awake.

Each one got out and, without saying a word, went straight to the men's toilet. Outside the pub we all stood around saying what a good trip it was and how well the car was running.

I could not look directly at any of the others and I don't think any of them looked at me.

I hoped they couldn't see just what I'd become and I didn't want to give myself away.

I led the way into the pub and ordered a squash instead of a beer.

The others mumbled that a squash sounded good to them and they'd have the same.

The barman was in a good mood and seemed grateful to have someone to break the loneliness of the outback pub.

As he made up four lemon squashes the barman asked how far we had come. We told him that we had come from Port Hedland and were heading to Meekatharra.

He asked us if we had passed the circus mob on the road.

Circus!

Circus!

What circus?

The barman told us that yesterday a circus had pulled into Kumarina. The manager had told him that they would camp somewhere up the road so the animals could stretch their legs.

The manager said that on a long trip the elephants were the ones who most needed a rest.

The elephants' legs suffered a bit on long trips.

He might think of camping the animals in the peaceful bush country for a day or so.

There was silence all around.

A silence you could cut with a knife.

The lemon squashes were slowly finished and the empty glasses put on the bar.

Comprehension dawned. Slow grins appeared on every face. A collective sigh of relief could be heard.

We all ordered a beer.

One sip of cold beer and we all started talking at a hundred miles an hour.

Each one of us had seen the elephant.

Each one thought the same thing I had thought.

Each one had decided to give up drink.

Each one of us had thought he had an alcoholic problem.

Each one was grateful that he was not the only one who had seen the elephant.

We finished our middies and ordered half a box of cold ones for the road. It was a four-stubby trip to Meekatharra.

I got behind the wheel with the greatest feeling of relief.

As we took off from Kumarina I had a serious thought.

Thank goodness we were not alcoholics.

Christmas
and Jack

Yelma Station had been home to the Ashwin family for many years. Arthur Cranbrook Ashwin had come from somewhere in South Australia. He had left behind a family and had ended up in Western Australia where he took up a pastoral property. He first owned the Banjawarn Station, then Dardar, then Wonganoo and, finally, Yelma. His homestead was near where Doyles Well is now.

Arthur ran cattle on the property and, while he paid for a substantial lease, his beasts roamed over an area of more than a million acres. He ran cattle from the Lake Violet Homestead boundary to the edge of Lake Carnegie, down as far as Deleta nearly to Lake Wells.

Arthur took up with a full-blood Tjuparn woman named Telfer. His children from Telfer were reared on the station and, along with others of the Tjuparn mob, had learned to work the property. Eventually he married Telfer.

Arthur and Telfer had two sons, Jack and Bill, and four daughters, Winnie, Trilby, Ida and the youngest one, Christmas Eve — who was born on Christmas Eve. She was the spoiled tomboy of the family. Winnie, Trilby and Ida were taught to be ladies by their mother and had to conduct themselves in a manner befitting the daughters of a station owner. Christmas could get away with anything but murder and from some of the things I've been told I can't be sure of that either. She could ride anything with hair and could beat even the toughest of the young men in a fair fight — but Christmas never fought fair anyway, she only knew how to win.

Winnie, who had several children to Scotty Dunn, died and the children were sent to Sister Kate's home for quarter-caste kids. Scotty Dunne took up a lease about forty miles south of Wiluna. Trilby married a bloke called Tom Cooper when he returned from the First World War. He was a very good horseman and had been with the Australian Light Horse at the charge at Beersheba — he became the manager on Yelma Station. Ida married a bloke called Archie Tucker.

Ashwin died sometime in the early thirties and after the funeral Telfer moved into Leonora, and Ida, Archie Tucker and Bill moved into Kalgoorlie.

The Ashwin children were all yellafellas and the government of the day did not allow people who were of mixed Aboriginal–European blood to own property. The family came under the 'protection' of the Aboriginal Protection Board and with the death of their father went from being property owners to being wards of the state — answerable to the Protector of Aboriginals.

However, before he died Ashwin had made a will and the Aboriginal Protection Board wanted to be seen to be doing the right thing by the Ashwin family. Arrangements were made for each of the children to receive some money from the sale of the property. Tom

Cooper and Trilby travelled to Kalgoorlie with the whitefella Protector representative to get the cheques, which were to be paid to each of them.

Jack was asked to stay at Yelma until the new owners came to take over and he kept sixteen-year-old Christmas with him for company. When the new owners came they would both travel into Wiluna where they could get jobs.

WHILE THEY WERE WAITING for the bloke from the Protection Board to return with the new owners, Jack and Christmas kept busy, moving cattle onto good feed and water. They got to talking about what the future might hold for them now their father was dead and they had lost the station. Jack told Christmas that the government bloke was sure to take advantage of them because neither of them could read nor write. They both agreed they would surely be robbed of what was rightfully theirs. They both thought they might as well get something worthwhile from the place before the government bloke returned with the new owners.

They got their good camp horses and began to gather as many cattle as they could. They herded them together around Cooper's Claypan and the saltbush area and worked hard for about two weeks by which time the mob consisted of about three hundred prime beasts.

Christmas and Jack

It was getting close to the time for the new owners to arrive along with the government Protector bloke. They decided to shift the mob off Yelma property and move it along the road towards Wiluna.

Together they pushed them onto Lake Violet Station. About fifteen miles into the property was the outcamp of Soak Creek. Jack told Christmas to stay and hold the mob around Soak Creek while he went back and waited for the new owners and the government bloke to finalise the takeover.

This story is easier to tell around a campfire over a couple of beers. Then some old stockman would scratch his head and note that there were only two people gathering over three hundred head of store bullocks, which is no mean feat in itself. A good stockman would also realise that the older brother, Jack, had left a sixteen-year-old girl to keep three hundred head of prime bullocks together for a couple of weeks without losing a beast. Well, Christmas did this on her own and never thought it was anything more than normal. She was so used to obeying her big brother that she simply performed the impossible as if it were an everyday occurrence.

Now OLD ARTHUR ASHWIN was a person who loved horses. In his young days in South Australia he said that jockey, poet and politician, Adam Lindsay Gordon, of Mt-Gambier-Blue-Lake-fame, was a

frequent visitor to the family home in Adelaide. Ashwin himself used to ride in steeplechases and always had first-class horseflesh. He bought beautiful Arab horses and bred them on his properties. Even today, out the back of Yelma and Windidda, down around the Deletta area, many these horses roam wild and free. They are the offspring of the old Kumbarari breed that Arthur bred. Sometimes, even today, if a person is lucky, one might see a magnificent iron-grey stallion leading his broodmares and foals into water. If you are lucky enough to encounter some of these beautiful horses, have a kind thought for the old man who brought such magnificent animals to this bush country.

So, Jack left Christmas at Soak Creek and returned to Yelma. When the new owners and the Aboriginal Protection bloke arrived they acted very contented with themselves, having made a good deal.

Christmas and Jack

The bloke from the department was all smiles as he handed Jack his share of the money for the property. Jack received fifty pounds and Chrismas got twenty-five pounds because she was not yet twenty-one. Jack played the game, 'poor-fella-blackfella-me' and showed proper respect for the government man. Like a good blackfella he showed the proper appreciation for having been ripped off for a prime property that at the time was more than a million acres.

'Where's Christmas, Jack?' asked the government man.

'She just got on her horse and rode to Wiluna,' Jack said. 'She's young and flighty and has a boyfriend in town that she wanted to see — she didn't want to wait around.'

'OK,' the government man said, accepting the explanation, 'will you take the twenty-five pounds for her?'

'Sure,' Jack promised, 'I'll start off for Wiluna tomorrow morning, but I'll need a horse to ride to town — it's well over a hundred miles from Yelma to Wiluna.'

They mumbled under their breath for a bit then reluctantly told him, 'Take your pick of the horses but don't take any of the blood stock.'

Jack chose an old mare and told them, 'She's a quiet old thing and I'm used to her. She's getting on in age and the new owners won't miss her — they've got the new Arab stallion and some blood mares for future stock.'

In the morning Jack rode off towards Wiluna on the old mare. Being a poor blackfella he didn't think it was important to tell them that the horse he was sitting on was an Arabian broodmare and that she was in foal to a splendid, valuable entire, or stallion. He rode slowly towards town with some very expensive horseflesh inside the mare's belly.

Jack rode to Soak Creek and gave Christmas her cheque. Like any good native girl she was grateful for the kind benevolence shown by the new owner and thankful that she had a kindly Aboriginal Protector to care for her interests and wellbeing.

Jack and Christmas gathered the mob together and pushed them slowly towards Wiluna. The mob was a mixed lot, having big old pikers and great stags to keep the young mickies in order, and they poked and watered and fed them towards town.

They drove the mob towards Wiluna and then veered in a southerly direction towards their brother-in-law's — Scotty Dunn's — property. Scotty made them very welcome and allowed them to hold the cattle on his block.

They let the mob mingle with Scotty's cattle. At the time there were a few thousand miners working on the Wiluna gold mine and it was a large town, which boasted two slaughter yards, a number of market gardens and a large piggery. Jack got a job as a slaughterman. Christmas stayed on the property and supplied the butcher with prime killers. She drove about ten bullocks to the slaughter yards every week.

⌒

JACK GOT MARRIED AND Christmas met a drover called Sandy Harris who had come down the Canning Stock Route from Halls Creek. A few years later they married and Christmas became known as Mrs Eva Harris. Under that name she became a legend in her own lifetime. They had a daughter and son, and that son was me. There are many more stories yet to be told about this remarkable person.

The old broodmare had a son as well. He grew up to become a very good racehorse and stood at stud in the district. His progeny can still be found on stations around Wiluna.

The
Bachelor

Us mob all worked at Boogoodoo Station for the last ten months mustering cattle. We all came into town for the races. Pedro was a young Aboriginal lad about twenty and had grown up on the station. When his father had died and his mother found another man, all of us on the station sort of adopted him and he became part of the station property along with the horses and the cattle. He couldn't read or write and only had a working knowledge of some sort of station-English.

Before coming to town we had warned the boys to be careful with those sheep-station jackeroos. The head stockman said, 'Those sheep-station jackeroos are a cheeky lot so keep clear of them. Ignore them if you can but don't take any rubbish either.'

We went to the races and some of the lads started drinking during the afternoon. Pedro made friends with a couple of young sheep-station jackeroos from Perth way and seemed to be staying out of trouble. We older blokes headed to the pub as the sun was going down. Several of us were under the weather by eight o'clock and well on the way to getting plastered. Pedro staggered in about half past eight and had blood all over him.

'What happened to you?' I asked.

'Had a fight with one of those jackeroo blokes,' he said.

I was surprised because they had seemed to have been getting along when I last saw them. 'That head stockman was right,' he said, 'that sheep-jackeroo got cheeky after we'd hada a few drinks.'

I asked him what had happened to cause a blue.

'When we got to the single men's quarters that young whitefella — that sheep-jackeroo from Perth — called me a "bechellus". I don't know very much English but it sounded like swearing to me, so I punched him,' Pedro said. 'I let fly just to be on the safe side and he hit me back and we had a pretty tough couple of minutes before we ran out of wind.'

I asked Pedro where this had occurred and he told me it happened at the single men's quarters. I asked him to repeat the rude word that young fella had said and he said it was the word 'bechella'. I scratched my head for a minute to clear the cobwebs and beer out of my brain and soon put two and two together.

'I don't think that fella was swearing at you. He must have called you a "'bachelor'",' I said. Pedro looked straight at me and assured me that that was the exact word that the bloke used and it was a good thing I could speak better English that he could.

I burst out laughing, loud and long. When I'd settled down, I explained that his mate was not swearing or saying anything bad.

I told him the word 'bachelor' meant the same as 'kitiji' in Martu talk. The jackeroo meant that he was single, or an unmarried man.

Pedro's eyes opened wide as he realised he'd punched the poor fella for nothing.

'I'm sorry for punching my new mate,' he said. 'I'd better go back and apologise.'

He grabbed a bottle of whisky and made his way back to the single men's quarters.

I smiled and ordered another beer. I reckoned I'd done my bit for reconciliation that night and I deserved a cold one.

The Runaway

The town was a small one on the southern edge of the vast, empty northern desert. There was a pub and general store that also served as a post office and petrol depot. There was a small school with about thirty pupils. It was a place where the Aboriginal people from several tribes gathered in small numbers. This number grew to several hundred people during the tribal Lore gatherings. There was a police station that had a sergeant and two constables. The police had an easy time for most of the year but things could become busy during the influx.

In the town lived several local Aboriginal families. Their children went to the local school. One yellafella, named Bronco, worked for the store and did some part-time work at the pub. Occasionally he got paid for helping the local police as a sort of black tracker and interpreter when some of the visiting tribal folk got into difficulty. Some of the families had arrived from the desert country only ten or so years ago and they lived in camps on the outskirts of the town. One particular family had a mother, father, two sons in their twenties, and a daughter. One son was named Smiley and the other one Togo. Smiley had a happy nature and laughed and joked with everyone. Togo was a quiet, pleasant chap.

At the time of this story some three hundred visitors had turned up for the Lore ceremonies and were camped about fifteen miles away where the ngurlu grounds (sacred grounds) were. This was a happy time. Some of the marlurlu (initiates) came from more than a thousand miles away. The Lore ceremonies could go on for several weeks. It was also a time for the exchange and promising of wives.

Some visitors used to go the pub and became nuisances when they had too much to drink. The police usually took them out to the camp in the paddy wagon where they could sleep off the strong drink. Sometimes a few would have to spend the night in the local lockup and receive a nominal fine or a caution from the local JP the next morning.

One morning the police pulled up at Bronco's house and asked to speak to him. The sergeant told him that there had been a fight out at the big camp and someone had been killed. The culprit had run off into the bush. The police would need Bronco's services for a few days. Bronco got into the police wagon and they drove out to the big camp. When they got there they began piecing the story together from what the witnesses told them.

A certain pretty young woman was the promised wife of one of the visiting young fellas but another bloke had already claimed her for himself. The fella who'd claimed the girl had only recently come in from the desert country. He lived and travelled around the edges of the great desert hundreds of miles to the north-east of the town. He was a half wild blackfella. When he wanted something or someone he just took it.

He was angry that the girl he wanted had been promised to another fella and he caused a big row. Spears were thrown. The wild bloke ended up spearing the young fella, killing him. Then he grabbed the girl and ran away. One of his cousins had gone with the murderer and the abducted young woman. The tracks led straight over the sandhills, up along the creek, and across the large flat country that led to the hills and bush country.

The wild fella was named Mangawarri, his cousin was Duarri and the girl was Barndigarra.

The police decided that the murderer had to be brought back with the cousin and the girl. The sergeant got Bronco and two constables together to give chase. Bronco asked the sergeant if Smiley should be included in the party. Smiley had only recently come in from that desert country and still had an intimate knowledge of that country to the north and east. He would be a valuable asset.

The party took off that afternoon before the runaways got too far ahead. Bronco and Smiley took the lead and quickly picked up the tracks where they'd crossed the large flat area beyond the long sandhills. The sergeant and two constables followed carefully behind and brought a good quantity of provisions. The tracks led straight north for fifty miles then veered to the east.

Bronco and Smiley kept on the tracks. They worked out that Mangawarri walked behind the girl, probably poking her along with a spear to make her hurry. Duarri walked several hundred yards to the right keeping a lookout for any pursuers. The tracks led onwards to where a whitefella named Macdonald had a camp. Macdonald was a sandalwood cutter and lived and worked mostly on his own. The police party came to the camp in the late evening and Macdonald told them that the group had called in and asked for some food. He gave them a feed and some food to take with them. Mangawarri told him that he had a new wife and he was taking her back to his own country because he didn't like town life. He told Macdonald his cousin would stay with them for a while and return later to live in town. The police group decided to camp the night and continue the next day.

In the morning Bronco and Smiley followed the tracks almost in a straight line north but lost them at a granite outcrop. Bronco and Smiley told the police to make a camp for a while and give them a chance to find the tracks again.

The two trackers walked in a wide circle around the granite outcrop and still could not find where the fugitives had come off the flat rock area. Towards evening they returned to the camp and told the waiting police that they'd lost the tracks. Both Bronco and Smiley were good trackers and were shamed to admit they had lost the tracks. They'd circled the country for miles and the only tracks they saw were Macdonald's, from when he had searched for sandalwood.

They'd seen where Macdonald had come over the granite country and walked into the flat watercourse country where there was plenty of sandalwood. Macdonald's boot tracks were the only fresh tracks that came off the rocky ground and had been going towards the north-west of where the camp was. They decided to camp that night and continue the next day and pick up the tracks of the three runaways.

That night Bronco had trouble sleeping. He was an experienced tracker and had a reputation to live up to. He was worried that he'd lost the tracks of three people and felt a little sad that he may have let the party down. He got up around one o'clock in the morning and made a billy of tea. As he sat back with the tea he was joined by Smiley who couldn't sleep either. Smiley got his mug of tea and sat next to Bronco. They sat silently for a long while. Finally Smiley looked up at Bronco and asked, 'What's wrong with us, we must be missing something.'

'We should both have a good rest tonight and have another try tomorrow,' Bronco told him.

Early the next morning, long before the sun came up, Smiley walked out to the place where the three people had walked onto the large granite surface. He went over the surface until he came to where the tracks of Macdonald came off the hard surface and went towards the wash country. He noticed that old Macdonald's tracks went in a north-west direction, almost in a straight line. Smiley knew of a waterhole that was about twenty miles away in that direction. It was the only place with a sure supply of water. He had a closer look at Macdonald's track and began to smile to himself as the solution slowly came to him.

He returned to the camp in time for breakfast and told Bronco that he had solved the mystery.

After the party finished breakfast he took Bronco and the police over to the granite flats. He pointed and said, 'Those boot tracks are very close together. The strides are much shorter than those Macdonald would make with his long stride. That runaway mob must have made the girl walk in front. The strides were the length a woman would take.'

The two men walked in her tracks, stepping carefully where she had trodden. What looked like the track of one person was really the tracks of three people walking in line, one after another. The last person was the person wearing Macdonald's boots — they had walked carefully covering the tracks of the two people before him. Bronco burst out laughing and Smiley joined in.

The sergeant came up to them to find out what they were laughing at. He must have thought they'd both gone mad. Bronco told the policemen what had happened and how they'd been fooled for a whole day. 'But don't worry too much,' he said, 'there's only one place they can be heading for. We can get in the police vehicle and drive straight there — to the next waterhole.'

And this is what they did.

When they reached a pool of water about twenty miles further on they found the tracks again where they must have had a drink before moving on. They were about half a day behind the runaways. Sergeant made Smiley the leader of the party — he was acknowledging that Smiley was the true expert in his own country and they'd follow his lead.

While the police party was having lunch Smiley sat back with his mug of tea and gave his opinion on what they should do next.

'The next water is about another twenty miles almost due north, in the direction Mangawarri wanted to go,' he said. 'Over to the east is some rough ranges country about fifty miles away. Up in the roughest part of the ranges is a cave with a permanent supply of water. My father showed me that small spring when I was only a small lad.

I've not forgotten it and three people could live there for a long time and never be found. I reckon Mangawarri would know about it too. And instead of going on to the obvious place with water he would veer east and do the unexpected.'

Smiley said the team should drive straight north and come around to the northern side of the ranges and approach the hidden spring from there. 'We can wait there for a couple of days and when Mangawarri and his friends get there we can catch them easily. Mangawarri is a proper warrior and a real cunning bugger,' he said and smiled, 'I'm a cunning bugger too.'

The police party decided that Smiley was indeed a clever bloke and they would follow his suggestion. The two four-wheel drive vehicles proceeded, passing the ranges away from the track the runaways would have to take. They went north of the ranges and turned in a wide circle to bring them into position. They made camp in a deep, wide creek that ran down from the hills.

They woke up in the early morning and after breakfast went up to the cave with the spring. They worked out that Mangawarri and his two companions could travel the fifty miles in about eight or nine hours. They would reach the cave around five o'clock that afternoon. The police group didn't go anywhere near the cave so as not to leave tracks. Bronco and the two constables took up positions above and to the left of the cave and Smiley and the sergeant took a position where they could watch the approach to the cave and have a view south, overlooking the path along which Mangawarri would arrive.

They waited in the deep shadow of a large overhanging rock so the sun would not reflect off anything they carried. The sergeant had his binoculars handy. He had a clear view of the spring in the mouth of the cave and the area where Mangawarri could try to escape. If he tried to run away he would run straight into the arms of Bronco and the two constables. They had them covered on all sides and expected they would be exhausted and thirsty after travelling fifty miles.

They waited quietly all day. They began to get anxious around four o'clock and had a drink of cold water and sat back while the sergeant checked his firearms.

The sergeant kept watching the back trail with his binoculars and suggested that maybe Mangawarri had outguessed them and taken another direction. Smiley looked at him with a grin and said he was very sure Mangawarri would come this way. 'I would have done exactly the same thing,' he said. And Sergeant thought it was only appropriate that they should use a dingo to catch another dingo.

IT WAS NEARLY FOUR-THIRTY when the sergeant spied the three approaching about a mile away. It was uncanny how Smiley was able to estimate this, almost to the minute.

'Mangawarri won't look around very carefully. They've been hurrying all day and are hungry and thirsty — the only thing they'll be thinking of is the cool water in the cave. Mangawarri won't expect anyone to be in these ranges — everyone has either died or moved into towns. There are no more people living out in this desert country,' he told the group. 'He'll feel safe out here and will become careless,' he said.

Very quietly and slowly Smiley and the sergeant moved into position so they could cover the progress of the three as they approached the cave. The spring fed into a small pool of water that reached to the mouth of the cave. Mangawarri was the first one to reach the water. He went down on his hands and drank straight from the pool. Duarri came next and then the weary young girl who lay on her stomach to drink. Smiley and the sergeant could see the two constables and Bronco standing back in the rocks on each side of the cave.

The sergeant gave the signal to stand back, took aim and fired a shot. The bullet landed next to Mangawarri. It made a spurt in the sand about a foot to his left. Sand flew up and in the confines of the small gorge the .303 sounded like a cannon going off.

Mangawarri jumped high into the air and then stood very still. The other two just lay as flat as they could on the ground. One of the constables loudly ordered Mangawarri to stand still and not move. The two constables moved out and put handcuffs on him and Duarri. The girl just lay there shaking with fright. Bronco moved to her side and spoke kindly, telling her not to be afraid. 'You'll be back with your family soon where you will be safe again,' he said.

The sergeant and Smiley came down and the sergeant moved everyone down to the police vehicles. A meal was soon put together and after a bit of a rest the party began the long drive back to town. Mangawarri accused Bronco of helping the police but Bronco said, 'This time Smiley should get all the credit for catching you.'

When they got back to town the sergeant and his two constables were full of praise for Smiley. He said if they ever needed a tracker in the future that Bronco should always include Smiley in the party.

Bronco praised Smiley to everyone he spoke to and told them that Smiley was a better tracker than he would ever be.

Tjoornoo
(waterhole, pronounced 'choornoo')

We were mustering horses on Wongawol Station, near Wiluna, and early one morning we caught and saddled up our good gallopers. Only horses that could keep a steady gallop or canter for an hour or so would be good enough for that day. We rode along the main creek and followed it up to where it started way in the ranges.

I was one of the younger blokes and followed the lead of the more experienced riders. I was not a good brumby runner like the others but I could certainly sit on a galloping horse without falling off.

Although, I must admit that I have bitten the dust more times than I like people to know — I've ploughed up my share of gravel with nearly every part of my body. I've connected my head with the ground so often that it could be a legitimate excuse for some of my queer behaviour in later years.

The particular day I want to tell you about was very clear. A blue sky, not a cloud anywhere. Nice and crisp in the early morning and a cool gentle breeze all day.

It was midday and we were into the ranges, looking out over the flat country. Up and up into the rocky country following the creek right to the top of the high country. We had followed the creek up to a bend where there was a spring with plenty of water. I did not know this spring was there. I had been on the station for about six months and no-one had said anything about this spring. Seeing it for the first time I got a feeling that somehow I had missed something. Surely someone would have mentioned that this water was here. In this country, letting people know where good water is to be found is as normal as breathing. Being a little bit manjong I didn't ask why I had not been told before of this lovely spring with good water in it.

Up until then we had not seen any sign of horses. No fresh tracks at all, only heaps of very old horseshit, or gurna, which told us that there had been a stallion in this area once, but a long time ago. The older blokes decided that we would have dinner camp here and then ride along the top of the ranges and follow another creek back to the main camp later.

Being the latest newchum I wanted to impress the older blokes and quickly rushed around gathering wood for the dinner-campfire. I expected one of the other young blokes would go to the spring and fill the quart pots with water for the tea. I had the fire going good and after awhile I asked that young bloke to go for the water. The other blokes had loosened the saddle girths on the horses and were sitting back under the shade of the trees. They looked at me strangely and one old bloke explained to me that they could not go for water. He said I was the only one who could.

'Whoa there bullock,' I thought, 'I might be the new bloke but I was not going to be taken advantage of by these fellas.'

The oldest of the blokes took it on himself to explain to me, very patiently, 'This particular water belongs to your tjamu, your grandfather. It's a special place, called Tjoornoo, and that's why no-one ever mentioned it to you. It's a place that's never mentioned lightly and is held in awe by everyone but, because you're a grandson, it's all right for you to get water from this spring. You should go down to the water and stand close and shout out to let the old fella know that you're a grandson and that you want water. After you get your water, then the others can get water for themselves. Be respectful because that old fella was very sulky and cheeky and easily upset. That water is sacred to the memory of that old fella's spirit, which still lives in the water. That particular tjamu had been a very powerful mabarn man and his memory is not to be taken lightly.'

I was quiet for a few minutes. I looked at the others to make sure they were not pulling my leg or having a go. Their faces looked serious enough so I picked up my quart pot and went down to the water.

As I got close I felt cynical and decided that what they said was ridiculous and they were having a joke with me because I was a new fella. I filled my quart pot and had a drink. I sat for a while and decided to see if what they said was true. I gave a shout and called out to that old fella, my tjamu, that I wanted water. I shouted loudly and, when nothing happened, I got braver. I picked up a rock and skimmed it across the water. I called out, 'If you can hear me you should wake up and say something.' Then I called out to the other blokes to come and get their water.

They came down to the water very carefully and scowled at me. 'You should have more respect for tjamu's memory or he might do something to you,' one fella said.

'He's already dead and he's useless now,' I said as I picked up some more flat stones and skimmed them across the pool. 'I dare you to do whatever you want,' I yelled. The other blokes looked at me and took off as fast as they could go — they didn't want to get punished for my actions.

We finished our lunch and rode along the top of the ranges and down another creek heading back to the main camp. It was about ten miles back and we didn't want to waste any time. As we came down onto the flats, still with about eight miles to go, I noticed a small cloud in the sky.

When we reached the flats I noticed a few more clouds. They were larger and darker and heavy with rain. We rode on for a few miles. Then the rain started. It came down in buckets and soon we were soaked to the skin. Nobody had thought to bring a raincoat because there had been no sign of rain that morning. The other blokes were looking at me in an accusing way — looking daggers at me. A couple were mumbling and blaming me for stirring up the old man's spirit. They said I should have let the old man rest in peace and not made him angry. It was a long ride home in the rising water and the mud that soon covered the flat ground. The horses were slipping and sliding and I got the feeling they too were blaming me for causing the heavy rain.

When we finally got back to camp it didn't take long for the story to go round and reach the others in the camp. Needless to say I was ostracised for a good week. Nobody wanted to be associated with me — I'd disrespected my long dead tjamu and my very own spring of water.

Someday I'd like to go back, find that spring in the ranges and apologise to my long-dead grandparent for behaving the way I did. I think he would understand and forgive me.

Dead Man Walking

Miserable, dreary, godforsaken country, this place. I was working at old Carnegie Station and the sun was so hot I felt like I was sitting in front of a blast furnace. I was born and bred in the bush country and had never seen a blast furnace, but the name seemed to fit. It was truly hot enough to fry an egg on a shovel. That was only supposed to happen in Marble Bar. Although I reckon that mob moved up there because the weather was better than here. The sun beat down with a savagery that made me think someone up there hated me, hated this earth and hated this bloody station.

I wondered, slowly, lazily, why on earth any sane person would choose to live way out here. The air was so still even the willy-willies didn't have the energy to stir. No wonder that town mob reckoned we were a queer lot. Sometimes I wondered about that myself.

The flies were too lazy to fly. All they could do was a slow stagger between any bit of moisture or sweat. They would stare at a drip of sweat for half an hour, slowly contemplating, before raising the energy to stretch their proboscis to get a drink. At least there was peace from them blokes for a while. In a couple of hours the afternoon breeze would come up and the buggers would spring to life. They tried to wriggle into your eyes, ears, nose or anywhere at all looking for something to eat or suck up.

The dog lay under the groundsheet that I had stretched over a gurarda bush for a bit of shade. He did not seem to be breathing.

If he was alive he kept it a secret. I watched him and it seemed to take half an hour from breathe-in to breathe-out then he gave a small half-hearted squeaky yelp — all part of his doggy dream — and I knew he was not dead. Probably dreaming about those mongrel bitches in town that he enjoyed playing sniffy-tail with. A great tail-sniffer, was my dog. If he liked another dog he lifted his tail so high and proud anyone would think he'd smothered aftershave under it.

I tried to spit but all I could muster was a sort of dry paste. I couldn't spit it out so I wiped it off with the cleanest part of my dirty shirt sleeve.

Good station country they call it, and they reckon some whitefellas went overseas and fought and died for it. I reckon there was something wrong with a person leaving a good green country like England to come here. Just look at the bloody place now. My own mob in the towns and cities are marching for land rights and screaming for native title. I don't see any of them coming out here to live in this part of the landed estate. They wouldn't last a week out here where there is no Coles, no Centrelink, no bottleshop and, thank goodness, no bloody ATSIC.

If you got into trouble there is no Aboriginal Legal Service to hold your hand. There is no Aboriginal Medical Service if you felt a bit crook. The whole medicine box consisted of epsom salts to open you up and chlorodine to block you up. One old drover kept a tin of treacle just in case one of the blackfellas got sick.

I had been on this station for the mustering season. From March right through to November. Now it was the middle of January and I'd been nearly six weeks on my own.

After we had trucked the bullocks, all the riders had gone to town for pink-eye. Even the boss and his family had gone to Perth where the weather was cooler. Like a fool I volunteered to stay back and look after the place.

I had unshod all the plant horses and put them out in the spelling paddock. The saddles and leather gear was all greased with camel fat and kerosene.

I did a mill-run and all the tanks were full and the windmills were pumping.

All I had to do was sit around and scratch myself or read a cowboy book. Louis L'Amour and Zane Grey were my favourite writers. Those two blokes seem to be the only western writers who knew that a Colt revolver carries only six bullets and a bushman always counts his bullets. They also knew that you couldn't gallop a horse all day without a spell like you can with a motorbike. Both these blokes would have fitted in well out here. Although they seemed to like excitement so they would need to go to town for the races every now and then. There they could have a good bareknuckle with the ringers from the other stations. They could even test out that young copper in town. He came from down south and would give them a bit of hot curry — something to write about. I had already read half the books from the tea chest that stood in the men's quarters. Some people die of loneliness and boredom and yet solitude is supposed to be good for the soul. It is all up to the individual, I reckon. And I reckon, whether I worry about it or not, the sun will still get up in the same place it usually did.

I WAS SITTING ON the verandah at the men's quarters, looking out into the distance, across the dry flats with only rocks and gibber stones, into the distant haze where the mirage looks like water and shimmers so much that, if you look at it for too long, you start seeing strange things.

I just had a slice of salt brisket and a cold potato and was thinking of putting on the billy or having a drink from the waterbag when I saw something.

About a mile from the men's quarters was the start of a dry wash that ended up as a creek that ran into the Lake Country. Long-dead trees stood as solitary reminders of once-better seasons long since lost to too many droughts. They stood between the camp and the thicket that was the start of the dry wash.

Something moved down there. Something dark. Like the shadow of a tree branch in the wind. But there was no breeze or willy-willy, or wind of any sort. I must have imagined I'd seen a shape of some kind but it was gone. Could have been an emu or something.

I had a drink from the waterbag and enjoyed the spit I'd been waiting for. I went into the kitchen and put the billy on. A mug of tea would be good.

I still had a gut feeling that I had seen something and my mind wouldn't let it go. I had been in the bush long enough to know what a shadow was. I also had the bushman's long-sightedness that came from living where most things exist at long distances. If a bushman sees the swish of a tail in the scrub, a half a mile away, he knows if it is a cow or horse or some other animal. That thing I'd seen was out of place. It was there and it shouldn't have been there — and then it was not there. My gut told me that I was not seeing things.

What was it? An emu? I'd known lone emus to come in to water during the heat of the day. An emu? Could be. But where was the pilot? Every bushman knew that when an emu came in to water in the middle of the day it was usually accompanied by a pilot. That pilot was a crow. Emus approached slowly and hung back while they sent in the crow to scout. If it was safe the crow always signalled that all was clear.

Dead Man Walking

WHEN I WAS LITTLE I asked my old Gami why the crow gave the all clear even when it could clearly see a man waiting with a gun. Gami reckoned that the crow told the emu that because they were both birds they should stick together and be wary of men, because men kill birds and eat them. What the crow failed to remind the emu was that, even though emus ate grass, crows ate flesh — especially fat emu flesh. So when the crow gave the all clear he was hoping the man would kill the emu. Then brother crow could feast on the scraps. A fine feathered friend indeed!

I WENT BACK OUT onto the verandah and even though it was shaded the hot wind still scorched my skin. I sat for a while and squinted into the distance to where I thought I'd seen that shape. I sat on a cyclone bed and tried to find my place in a Louis L'Amour book. The billy had boiled so I got up and put in some tea-leaf. I put it aside to draw.

I stopped in the doorway and my mind registered that shape again. I saw something. Then it moved into my line of sight. It stood still, and it stood out clearly, as if it wanted me to get used to it being there. It was a man, just standing there. I began to panic and the hair stood up on the back of my neck.

As far as I knew the closest station was fifty miles away and there should not have been another human being around. It looked like an

ordinary man but then all the mamu stories from my childhood began to tickle my memory. Thoughts came rushing into my consciousness like a crowd of women at a jumble sale. Out in this country there is the story of the ngayurna ngalgu, a giant hairy man like the Big Foot in America. Blackfellas say they eat kids. I wondered: if one was hungry enough would he bother requesting a birth certificate? I knew that if I couldn't get lamb I could always chew on a bit of mutton. I suspected this ngayurna ngalgu wasn't particular about the quality of a bit of blackfella steak. Then again, this is Wanmalla country too. I had been reared up on Wanmalla stories. I didn't know if the stories were true or not but this was certainly not the time to find out.

I rubbed my eyes and tried to focus again. I could see the figure. It was definitely human — normal height, normal build. I tried to think of anyone I knew of who had gone missing or had gone mad — or maybe he was a mass murderer on the loose. There had been no mention of any homicidal maniacs on the loose on the radio. No mad lunatics or city crims. Not even someone normal who had become lost.

My dad had taught me to always be prepared — wherever possible, to be one step ahead of any situation. This certainly seemed to be a situation. Being a careful sort of bloke I moved into my room and pulled my .44 Winchester out of the cupboard. After checking that the magazine was full I laid it on the bed, within easy reach. I stood in the doorway and stared at the figure standing under that giji tree about five hundred yards away. Five hundred yards! Bloody hell! A .44 was no good at five hundred yards. It was only good for two hundred yards. I moved steadily back into the room and pulled out the good old .303 and filled the magazine. Any target that was over two hundred yards needed the old .303 to make sure of a hit. This done, I felt as if I was in control. I moved outside and sat on the cyclone bed, in the shade. I looked at a tree in the distance — about three hundred yards to the right of where I had seen him. This way I could keep him in my peripheral vision — this was a bushman's trick. If you stare directly at a distant object it can seem to move. I kept him in my vision this way and wondered who he was, why he was here and how he got here — it was beyond my understanding. Feeling safe with my two friends close within reach I made another cup of tea and sat down to see what developed.

The figure moved very slowly towards the watertank. He was letting me know that he'd come for water. In the bush nobody denied another person access to water. He moved as if there was something wrong with his left foot because it seemed to drag. Slowly he made it to the tank and stood on the yard rail so he could get to the water. He put his head down and had a drink and then looked around. It looked as if he was only having small sips, so I thought that he was certainly very thirsty. He was an experienced bushman who knew not to gulp down water when one was really thirsty. I sipped on my pannikin of tea.

He got down from the tank and was sitting in the open not far from the trough. My thoughts were running amok like a bolting half-broken colt. I had to put a short rein on them before I panicked and grabbed the rifle. He was sitting sideways on to me and looking at his feet. I had no intention of letting him out of my sight. We sat like that for about half an hour. I was getting impatient and wondering whether a .303 bullet next to his feet would provoke any action. Then he got up and sort of shuffled slowly and deliberately towards the gurarda bush where the dog was. Now that dog of mine was sitting with his ears up and was all but wagging his tail. The dog was not making any noise or fuss. I thought to myself that maybe the dog knew this bloke — he normally went berserk when strangers came too close but this was queer behaviour to my way of thinking. Taking a page out of my dog's book I relaxed a bit and moved to the end of the verandah. While sitting and thinking, my mind clicked over and I thought that this situation reminded me of traditional behaviour when a stranger approaches another person's camp. This man was waiting for me to make the next move. I should give him some sign of welcome so he could approach in peace. With this in mind I walked out into the area in the front of the quarters and sat on a large stone. We must have been separated by about twenty yards. He looked directly at me for a spell then he looked towards the way he had come and then put his head down. I decided it was my camp and it was for me to speak first.

I gave the hand signal and asked wayipa. He pointed towards the tank and said kapi, indicating that he had come for water. We had opened communications and indicated friendly intentions so I moved closer. I asked him where he had come from. He answered in hesitant pidjin that he came from the north, a long way. I asked his name and he faltered before he answered — it was as if it took a tremendous effort to identify himself. I had plenty of time so didn't push him. I got the feeling he was reluctant to say his name. Out in the bush country, men are quite often known by a name that is not the one their mother knows them by. The reasons for this are many, maybe a lost love affair or the wife took off, or maybe there are some warrants chasing them. After a few moments of silence he gave a sigh as if he'd made an important decision. He gave me a quick look to see if I was paying attention then dropped his eyes and looked at the ground before he spoke.

'I'm brother to that mugundu from Boogoodoo Station,' he said.

I told him, 'I know that bloke, he is uncle to me. My mother is Christmas from Yelma and Dardar.'

He looked at me and said that he knew who I was and added shyly, 'I know your mother and father too. When I was small I owned a donkey that you used to ride.'

We sat in silence for a while and I got the impression he was debating whether to say any more. We had followed the traditional protocol and both shown our willingness for company and our wish to communicate. I had the idea he wanted to say more but needed permission to speak. He seemed to have a hesitancy about him, which I found strange but which I accepted. My wirla, my gut feeling, told me he was begging for permission so, to give him some encouragement, I fell back on my horse-breaking experience. I had to do some 'bagging down', he had to settle. I asked him if he wanted some tea and he nodded. I went into the kitchen, made us both a pannikin and put his on the table. I told him to put in his own sugar and milk. He seemed to ponder what I had said to him as if he was not just trying to sort out my words but trying to put them in sequence so they made sense. He came up the steps slowly like a dog that'd been whipped too many times. He stood at the table and I passed the pannikin towards him. He gave me a look like he wanted me to give him permission to have something that had been forbidden for many years, for too long. I sipped my tea saying, 'It tastes very good and is just the best thing for a man on a hot day.'

This was a bit more 'bagging down'. Nothing like a good cup of tea to establish a good rapport with a person. Many a lasting friendship had been cemented over a good cup of Bushells in a dinted but clean-on-the-inside tin pannikin. He eventually took up his tea and we went out onto the verandah and sat down. He sat on the lower step a little way from me and remained alert like a brumby at the trough, ready to run at the first sign of danger.

I felt I was missing something. Surely a man walking in from the desert was not an everyday happening. I thought of my dad who said there were always stories within stories. I noticed that he had finished half his tea. He looked up at me like a turn-turnpa — young girl — seeking permission to address an Elder. I gave him a look of encouragement — the same look the world over.

He said he came from this country. I noticed he did not say that he 'belonged' to this country. I wondered at the choice of words but thought that an explanation would come eventually. Then he said that his people belonged to this country. I gave him that look which asks for an explanation.

He told me that once he had a woman. I was expecting this part, for where is there a good yarn without a woman involved, or a good dog or a good horse? This woman had been the promised wife of another man. She had been promised to an older man from when she was turn-turnpa. There had been an altercation of some sort. He did not elaborate and it was not for me to ask for particulars. Sometimes the less said the better. The eternal triangle knows no boundaries. I was not one to enter into the secret places of a man's heart. A man's soul is his personal possession. His sacred place. This bloke had his own dreaming to sort out in his own way.

In this case the husband had been killed and my new friend had run away with the woman. There was no need for him to tell me that the woman had been the wrong skin for him. If she had been the right skin there would not have been a story. The mob, that is, the dead bloke's brothers and the woman's brothers, had not caught the two runaways. He told me they'd gone away, out into the desert, beyond the last lake and even beyond that country. I tried to work out where that distant lake was supposed to be. I had never been that far but had heard stories from some old people and travellers who told me about that lake.

'There was a child,' he said, 'born way out beyond the Lake Country, but it died. When the next drought came my woman died. I've lived alone ever since.'

He told me that sometimes he came close to the station and watched the musterers going about their work. He said he was once a good rider and missed the mustering.

I invited him to stay awhile and keep me company. He dropped his head and looked at the ground. It seemed a long time before he answered. He gave a sad sigh of resignation and said, 'I can never come back. I'm a dead man. I have no name. I do not exist. I have been wiped from the memories of my friends and family. It is as if I had never been born.'

In Aboriginal Lore there were many forms of punishment for misbehaviour. These ranged from mild verbal censure to physical punishment sometimes requiring serious injury or death for the perpetrator. I had witnessed some of these punishments from time to time. In classical Aboriginal society the ultimate punishment is not death. Nor is it spearing or beating the wrongdoer, which offers satisfaction to the person who has been wronged. Carried out formally and in accordance with the Lore the wronged person is appeased. The family is appeased and the community is appeased. Everyone is freed from individual or collective guilt. The people are cleansed, the earth is cleansed, the universe is cleansed. The whole Dreaming is cleansed and nature can return to orderly existence again. Once the rains come and the new grass comes up, new life can be born and the whole of nature is happy again.

But the ultimate punishment is ostracism, banishment from all human contact. The outcast is treated as if they were dead. Their name is no longer spoken. The memory of their existence is erased from everyone's mind. It is as if that person had never been born.

My new friend, sitting on my doorstep drinking my tea, took on a new persona. He was pleading for understanding. Not sympathy, he wouldn't do that, he was too much of a man for that. He only wanted me to understand.

But how could I understand what this bloke had been through? I felt for him but how could I even begin to put myself in his place? I had a large extended family. I had a place in the world. I had close friends to share my problems and my hopes with. It struck me that I'd thought being left alone on a station during the Christmas break was a raw deal. But I need never feel alone — I could always read a book and enter the pages and travel all over the world. I was able to read anything I wanted.

My heart beat slowly in contemplation. I tried to clear my mind and my heart in an attempt to get a feel for this bloke before me. All my bravado disappeared and my energy and compassion flowed out to this other soul who lived a life I probably could not survive. It was impossible for me to think that I could help him, I knew I couldn't take some of the load and ease his burden — not even just for a while. Where did this man get the will to live a life less than that which the almighty intended man to live — it was as if he had risen above this life. I felt that I was in the presence of a better man than I. He showed that he had greater wisdom and knowledge of humanity than I.

He told me one time he broke his leg and crawled into an isolated Aboriginal community where the nurses flew him to Alice Springs for treatment. This had been a few years back, and he still had a limp. He said that he had stayed in hospital for about a month and was flown back to the community and cared for by the local schoolteacher and his family. Only one old widow from the community talked to him while he stayed there. It seemed important that he had been in touch with other people even though the contact was all too brief.

He began to talk to me.

We talked well into the night and as we spoke some of his strength passed into me. His isolation had given him an understanding of humanity that went beyond that of any man I had met.

I offered him some tobacco. He accepted gracefully but said that he would mix it with jurnpa ash and make chew. Then I offered him a full tin of Log Cabin to take with him when he left. He thanked me and said it would last him a long time. He told me he wouldn't come to see me again, but if he was near he would shine the tobacco tin lid and I would know it was him and he was nearby.

WHEN I WOKE UP the next morning he had gone. He had washed his pannikin and hung it on its nail — all trace of him having been there had gone. I looked for his tracks but there were none to see. My new but temporary friend had gone back to join the mirages and willy-willies and the everlasting dust and far-off places of that country beyond the Lake.

THE YEARS HAVE GONE swiftly and I am a lot older now but I still have this yarn that I have told to only a few trusted friends. Sometimes when I am alone during the heat of the day, resting in the shade, I put down my book and look out towards the distant stony flats and across the mulga thickets. I look towards the distant mirage and whirls of dust. My eyesight is weaker now but if perchance I see the flick of something shining a long way off yonder, I wonder what it might be. Maybe a piece of crystal quartz or a piece of broken bottle glass glinting from the sun? Maybe. Or maybe it is the sun's reflection from the lid of a Log Cabin tobacco tin.

Rooftop
Refuge

Wiluna is a town at the western edge of the Western Desert. At the time of this story it had a large population of Aboriginal people who worked in a big orange orchard just out of town. On this particular Friday the first gang of orange pickers had been paid early and had already done their shopping. Among this group were Cowboy and Ned who had made their way to the pub. When the pub closes at ten o'clock most of the workers grab a box of beer and find someplace to have a party. As a rule, a mob usually ends up at Cowboy's and when they run out of their own beer they start drinking his.

This particular night Cowboy told them he hadn't bought any beer. But earlier on he had sent his wife Dillo home with a block of beer before the main force came into the pub. So he left the pub and walked home at about half past nine, slightly tipsy but without any extra grog.

When he got home he got Dillo to put the ladder against the roof and she climbed up. He passed a mattress and bedding — and the block of beer — up to her. By the time the pub closed they were very comfortable on the roof. Cowboy had his beer and his wife to talk to and he stretched out, very cosy, quietly sipping his beer. This was one night when he wouldn't have to put up with all the blackfellas turning up with a pile of grog and making noise, possibly fighting around his house and making general humbug for all the neighbours. The other advantage was that he had his own grog and smokes and didn't have to share them with that bludging mob. He climbed down the ladder a couple of times for a gumbu against the lilac tree in the corner of the yard before the pub closed and the rush started.

Sure enough, as soon as the pub shut a crowd began turning up at Cowboy's house. He lay back quietly and listened to them calling his name and inviting him to drink with them. His favourite mate, Ned, arrived first and called out around the house for a while. Then Bucksie and Ashie turned up and joined Ned. They drank a couple of cans while they waited for Cowboy to turn up.

Cowboy smiled to himself. He had finally found a way to get away from this noisy mob on pay night. He promised himself he would pull this trick more often.

The other blokes got tired of waiting around and agreed that Cowboy must have gone over to his other mate Lester's place for the night. They took off over to Bucksie's camp where they could shout, fight and talk as loud as they liked all night. They missed Cowboy because he could tell a good yarn over a beer and he could argue with the best of them. He would gladly accommodate anyone who wanted to go the full mile and have a fight. One good thing about fighting Cowboy was that if he was winning he would not put in the leather. When he knocked a person down he would open another can and have a drink while waiting for his fighting mate to get up.

When all the visitors had taken off, Cowboy opened another can and lay back, very satisfied with his plan. He dozed off for an hour or so. Dillo had gone to sleep as well.

Sometime during the night the intake of beer began to take effect again and he had to have another gumbu. He forgot he was on the roof and walked towards where the lilac tree should have been. He staggered towards the tree and suddenly there was nothing beneath his feet. Where the ground should have been there was just space. As he was falling he automatically crossed both arms to protect his face. He fell with a loud thud. When he hit the dirt all the weight went on his elbows. He shouted for help and Dillo came down the ladder and called the ambulance. At the hospital they found that he had broken both arms. His arms were both plastered and he was helpless for the next month or so.

None of his drinking mates felt sorry for him. They reckoned he had been punished for being selfish and trying to be smarter than everyone else. His mates had a quick look at each other, shook their heads and all agreed that surely, surely, 'Pride cometh before the fall'.

Blackfella Gaol

I was twenty-two years old when I first went to gaol. Up to this time I was a station blackfella. We were different to town blackfellas. We station blackfellas looked down on that mob and classed them as bludgers, no-hopers and gaol-birds. Of couse we were right too, the white boss said so.

Anyway, I found myself in prison. Of course I should not have been there; I was too good for gaol. I'd been in trouble with the town police before and the white boss had always bailed me out and paid my fines. He understood energetic young fellas who had been out on the station for six months and had steam to blow off. The JPs and magistrates were usually understanding and tolerant towards good station blackfellas. But this time was different. No slap on the wrist this time. In Queensland there was a mandatory sentence of six months for the third offence of driving a motor vehicle while under suspension, and this is what I got.

My mother was the only person who cried for me. My father said that it served me right for showing off to those town blackfellas with my brand new second-hand Holden ute. My sisters said it served me right because I'd let the station people down. My two older brothers said I'd been spoiled by Mum and it was about time I got what I deserved. My girlfriend refused to talk to me and began to look at the new jackeroo with sheep's eyes. I knew that look too, that was how she used to look at me. In one weekend I had changed from being an upstanding young stockman to being a blackfella gaolbird.

I was escorted along with three others to the big town on the gulf where the prison was situated. When we got there we were processed by the prison staff. My flash and colourful RM Williams stockman's clothes were exchanged for drab grey prison garb. That was when I really knew my life had changed. They say that 'clothes maketh the man' and now I knew just how true this was. I walked into the prison building one person and walked into the prison yard a different one altogether.

Straight away I was greeted by lations and mates. I was a 'cleanskin' and the old 'lags' and young blokes went out of their way to make me feel at home. One old fella, Uncle Simon, welcomed me and told me that I should put this down to experience and go and do something better with myself. He had been in and out of gaol for most of his adult life and had become resigned to that life. He told me to make it my first and last time in gaol.

Uncle Simon had gone to gaol when he was fifteen and was now about fifty-nine years old. Every time he was released he hit the grog heavily. He'd breached his parole that many times he'd given up hope of ever having a life outside of gaol. He took me under his wing and began to teach me the ropes; how to survive in prison. One thing he taught me was that I could choose whether to be happy or sad, miserable or glad. He told me to say the words out aloud. No matter what happened I was to say, 'That's good'. If a cyclone came and killed a lot of people he said that I should count the survivors and be happy, not brood on the number of people that died. 'Don't mourn too long for the old man who has just passed away,' he'd say, 'be happy for the newborn grandchild.'

He used to say no matter what happened today the sun would rise tomorrow. It would rise in the same place as it always did regardless of whether I was in a good mood or bad mood. The sun would set in the same place it always did, whether I liked it or not, whether the police liked it or not, whether the magistrate liked it or not, even whether the Prime Minister — or anybody in the white man's government — liked it or not.

Another very important lesson he taught me was that, when you're in prison, don't brood about anything that happens on the other side of that razor-wire fence. Don't worry about what my girlfriend was doing. Do not expect any phone calls or letters. Out there was another world over which I had no control whatsoever. He said, 'the world "out there" will go on whether you like it or not and there's nothing you can do about it. You can do "hard time" or "easy time" — "whitefella time" or "blackfella time".'

On the ladies' side of the prison at this time was a middle-aged woman known as Matron Dolly. She began her gaolbird career as a teenage girl who refused to get off the street after six o'clock when ordered by the police. This old town used to have a six o'clock curfew that said that natives had to be off the streets by then. The penalty for this offence was seven days in the local lockup. Matron Dolly's criminal record began with twenty-five straight convictions of this particular offence. She is very proud of her prison record and maintains that she might be a gaolbird but she is not a criminal.

Most of her later convictions were made up of the old 'native trifecta'. In Queensland the trifecta reads on the charge sheet as 'disorderly conduct' followed by 'resisting arrest' and culminating in 'assaulting a police officer'. The last charge can bring a sentence of anything from three to eighteen months. When blackfella gaol-birds see some relation or mate come to prison with these charges they know that some bad cop wanted to go nigger-bashing and, to make it look legal, resorted to using the trifecta. Old blackfella gaol-birds often tell the younger blackfella that he is safe in gaol. They tell them that it is dangerous for blackfellas on the outside.

Matron Dolly got her name because she had done some nursing when she was younger. When she's in prison she usually serves at sick parade, dosing medicine and bandaging cuts and bruises. She endeared herself to me from the very first by telling me to bring my outsized prison clothes to her. She took my measurements, undid the stitches and re-sewed the clothes to fit me as good as any tailor-made suit could be. I was now a smartly dressed gaolbird. She also took it upon herself to do my washing. As a result I was always dressed 'spunky fit' during my time in gaol.

THE PRISON HAD BEEN built by convicts sometime in the 1800s. It was made from stone and the bars and doors were hand-forged by blacksmiths. Along the north fence were ten two-man cells that still had the old bucket-toilet system. Along the west side was a large building like a high barn that had bars all around and could accommodate up to forty people. It was nearly always filled with blackfellas. This building was built at the time when there was a bounty on every blackfella brought into prison — the government of the day paid prisons a certain price per head. Depending on the numbers of prisoners in custody the person in charge could have a very lucrative second income. Especially if, when the prison officers took the trusted prisoners out to hunt and fish, they could bring in plenty of kangaroo meat and catch a lot of fresh fish to supplement the prison stores. The older blackfellas remember when there used to be nearly a hundred people jammed into that shed-like building. Being in charge of a prison was a good business in those early days.

After about four months into my gaol term I began to feel a little bit comfortable with the rest of the gaol-birds and the prison system.

In the cool afternoon we had about an hour to spend together before lock-up and I enjoyed the yarns from other blokes about things they had done and places they had been. Sometimes one of them would touch on what he would do when he got released. Some had a job to go to. Others had a wife and kids and a home to go to. Sometimes if a bloke was soon to be released on parole the other blokes took bets on how long it would be before he'd breach his parole and be back with us. 'Don't put his bedding away and keep his cell vacant because he'll be back on the weekend,' they'd say, or, 'he's going away on a short holiday and will be back soon.' There's a gaolbird brotherhood among men who have served time together.

At the beginning of the last month of my sentence I was looking at my release date getting closer and I began thinking about how the mustering on the station would soon be starting and how I might ask my father to pick me up at the prison gate the day of my release. I swore to myself that, when I was released, I wouldn't go to town for twelve months straight.

ONE PARTICULAR DAY ALL I had to do was wash two of the prison vans and get them ready for escort duty. In the late afternoon I wandered down to the end of the prison compound to the large shade of a big mango tree. There was a small group already there talking about everything, and nothing. A quiet joke here and a chuckle there. I sat down and leaned back against the trunk of the tree. I looked up and saw Uncle Simon beckoning me.

He was standing alongside the fence, which was made of seven-foot high roofing iron with razor wire on top. He had a serious look on his face and, with a stern voice, told me to stand near a certain white rock. He told me to stand with one foot on each side of that rock. Without thinking anything was strange I did as he instructed in a slow sort of way. He told me to keep a straight face and listen carefully. He told me not to frown, smile or make a comment in any way at all. I made my face blank and looked straight at him. When he was satisfied he said in a voice that would be the envy of any supreme court judge, 'Mr Douglas Mackenzie, your sentence is almost complete and the boys thought that they would give you a small going-away present. Under your feet, buried in the sand, there are two bottles of tawny port, one bottle of Bundaberg rum and two bottles of Johnny Walker Red Label Scotch whisky. There are enough cigarettes and tobacco to last you for the next month. You don't know where they came from. You don't know who put them there. You don't even try to thank any person at all. As a matter of fact you don't even know that they are there. Now, be a good boy and go and sit back under the tree and tell us gents all about the station you will be going back to.'

My cell had bars that came right down to the floor and had shutters that could be closed when a cyclone came. From the bars I could reach out and dig a hole in the sand and bury my bottles. Over the next week or so I carefully dug up all those bottles and buried them there, nice and close so I could keep a close eye on them.

At night I could reach through the bars and pull out a bottle, have a drink with my two cellmates and put the bottle back in the sand. No-one was any the wiser. We only touched them it was safe to do so.

Matron Dolly did work for the sergeant's wife down at the local police station. One afternoon she came back with the latest town news. It seemed someone had broken into the local co-op store and stolen a ton of grog along with cigarettes, tobacco, clothes and a large quantity of food. They must have been professionals because they also stole the store's delivery truck. Then they went on to rob the local pub and the mess down at the wharf. The pub had almost a truckload of alcohol stolen from the storeroom and a lot of cold stuff from the fridge. The mess at the wharf had all the alcohol stolen and most of the spirits and wine had been taken. The police were running all over town checking everyone out to try to find the culprits. They spent a long time up at the native reserve but everyone there was sober and all of them were out of smokes so it couldn't have been them, and the police couldn't get any information out of them anyway. Then they employed two of the local blackfellas to help track down the perpetrators.

Matron Dolly said most of the townspeople were in an uproar because they were the largest break-ins the town had ever had. She said she saw townsfolk running around everywhere in panic. Some even feared an invasion into their very home. Many were buying padlocks to lock their front gates, doors, cars and sheds. Almost everyone with a firearm had stocked up on bullets and was making preparations to defend their homes and family. Dolly was flustered and nervous when she was telling the folk in the exercise yard. She shopped at the local store and was friends with the store manager's wife. Sometimes she did house cleaning and babysat for them. She did the same for the publican's wife and was friendly with that family too. Dolly was very upset that some thoughtless and disrespectful mob had done this to her home town.

Uncle Simon listened carefully and very kindly put his arms around her and gave her a hug. He told her not to worry too much about it because the thieves would surely be caught soon enough.

He led her back to the entrance to the women's cells and on the way whispered to her that there was bottle of rum under her mattress in her cell to help her settle down. He said it would help her get a good night's sleep. He told her to use it for medicinal purposes only. He told her that an old lady of her age should not worry too much about what happened outside the prison walls. It was not our concern what the whitefellas did to each other. He was a very wise old man, our Uncle Simon; Matron Dolly knew it was always best to heed his sage advice.

THERE WERE STILL A number of us standing under the mango tree. Mostly smoking and talking quietly about insignificant things. Somebody coughed and when we looked up we saw five local police officers with two blacktrackers walking up along the beach towards the prison. They were supposedly following the tracks of the robbers. Suddenly every blackfella under that tree was looking at the ground.

Uncle Simon walked away from the main group. He stood out in the open where he could be seen by the trackers on the hill. No-one said a word. Uncle Simon looked straight at the two blacktrackers.

The trackers were inspecting the ground — looking at tracks that were leading straight to the prison fence. The policemen were searching around the trees and along the beach. They probably expected to see the robbers in the distance. They didn't look at the ground at all. That was blacktrackers' work. Whitefella policemen did not look down at the ground. The two professional trackers looked straight down at the fence topped with razor wire. They looked over into the prison yard. They looked at Uncle Simon who was standing alone in the open. They looked straight at him and he looked straight back. Every blackfella in the region knew Uncle Simon.

Both of the blacktrackers had served time in this gaol. Uncle Simon looked directly at them and, very slowly and carefully, he moved one hand. They dropped their heads and looked meaningfully at each other for a few seconds. After a quick nod from the older chap the younger bloke accidently missed his footing. He slipped and rolled down the sandy hill for quite a distance obliterating most of the footprints. When he regained his balance he stood up and the older bloke spoke to the policemen. It seemed that following the tracks was getting difficult. The group moved off along the top and then down the far side of the hill. Before the trackers' heads moved out of sight they turned and gave an almost imperceptible nod to Uncle Simon. Uncle Simon lifted a hand in silent acknowledgement.

He came back to the group and told us the young tracker was his cousin and the older one was his uncle. He said they would follow the tracks of the thieves along the beach for a distance and eventually lose them where the tide had washed them out. They would still get paid for their effort in assisting the police.

THE NEXT DAY DURING the afternoon break, before the evening meal, Uncle Simon called me over to where he was standing against the old cell block. He stood near one of the original steel doors and asked, 'Can you guess how the grog got in?'

'I haven't got the faintest idea!' I said.

'Have a look at the whole cell block and look at the doors. Do you notice anything wrong with any of the doors?' I looked hard but couldn't see anything out of the ordinary.

'Have you ever built a stockyard for holding cattle?' he asked.

'I'm a good builder,' I told him.

'How do you place the hinges for the gates so a bull can't put his horn under it and lift the gate off the hinges?'

'I always make sure that the top hinge faces down and the bottom hinge faces upwards so the gate can't be moved up or down.'

'You're a smart lad,' he said, 'and you should take another look at cell number three and see if there's anything wrong with the way it was built.'

I sat down near cell number three and rolled a smoke and looked out over the exercise yard. I slowly dropped my eyes to the hinges and held my breath for a long while. I could not believe what I saw. Both of the bolts holding the hinges on this particular cell faced upwards. A strong person could lift the cell door off its hinges and open it. Three strong blokes could put the cell door back on again and no-one would know.

I slowly looked into cell number three and looked straight into three pairs of the most innocent, angelic looking eyes that ever a priest or mother superior could look into. I carefully turned my head and looked at the ground. Us blackfellas were very good at looking at the ground. I scuffed the toe of my prison boots in the sand and slowly walked away from cell number three. In gaolbird language, my silent back walking away, straight and tall said it all. I was saying thanks to the contributors of my farewell drinks.

The next day most of the inmates quietly went about their business. Three of us went out to get some chairs with one of the prison officers. When we came back to the prison we ran into the biggest crowd of drunken blackfellas in the exercise yard. Some were arguing, shouting and throwing punches. Others were wrestling on the ground.

The prison officers could not control this mob and some went to call in the local cop to lend a hand. When they went to the office to phone for help, the warden, Mr Middleton, asked what the trouble was. The young officers told him there was a riot in the yard and they needed help to control those unruly blackfellas. Old Mr Middleton had been in charge of this gaol for over thirty years. He gently told the officers to settle down and not to panic. He said he would go out and see what the matter was with his boys. To the blackfella inmates, this stately old gentleman had been carer and benefactor — to a great number he had been like a godfather for most of their adult lives. They respected and revered the old man.

As the old man walked out into the yard everyone fell silent. He spoke as gently as a priest taking confession. He asked them to quietly get into a parade line-up. The men immediately fell into three lines. Some of them were so drunk they were tripping over themselves, and several had to be held up by their mates — but they all tried their best to stand to attention. Mr Middleton walked slowly along the lines, up and down and through again. The poor old fella was almost overcome by the alcoholic fumes — there was no doubt in his mind what the problem was.

The story of the recent spate of robberies was common knowledge among the prison staff and it didn't take him too long to put two and two together. It all fell into place and as he walked among the lines you could have heard a pin drop.

He quietly told the boys to go back to their cells and sleep it off. He said he would see them, one by one, the next day. Then he ordered them to bring what remained of the grog up to the office.

I STOOD WITH MY two cellmates and watched in awe at the amount of grog brought forward. We couldn't have imagined where some hiding places had been. The young prison officers might have thought they knew all there was to know about this gaol but this blackfella gaol sure gave them, and me, an education.

The next morning during rollcall Mr Middleton addressed the assembly. He said he didn't want to know the names of the perpetrators. He didn't want to know how the miracle had happened that 'blackfella manna' fell from heaven into his prison yard.

'I'm going to confiscate all the alcohol,' he said, 'and the tobacco will be put in your property cabinets and retrieved in the same way. I will forget what happened here and it will not leave the prison — whatever happens inside these prison walls stays inside.'

Of course I was an innocent bystander and definitely not a hardened gaolbird. At the time of the riot I'd been carting chairs and in the company of two prison officers. There was no alcohol on my breath. I didn't have any excess tobacco in my cell. There was no alcohol found in my cell.

THE NEXT WEEK A golf tournament was held over the weekend. All the local businessmen and station owners attended the tournament and on the Sunday afternoon they gathered at the home of the prison warden. Those who had won trophies were presented with cups and assorted items to show they had done well at golf. Mr Middleton was president of the local golf club. Among the distinguished guests were the main leaders of the town. The manager of the local cooperative store and gallon license, the Inspector of Police and the two sergeants, along with several senior constables, the manager of the local wharf, the owner of the hotel and bottleshop, the local magistrate and several justices of the peace, and many of the shop and store owners and pastoralists — they all attended this august gathering.

The warden's residence was one of those buildings common in the tropics and warmer climates. It stood on seven-foot steel stumps and the floor and verandah stood higher than the perimeter fence of the prison so the warden could look out and over the prison yard. In the early evening, with the prison in darkness, the bright lights of the warden's party were in full sight of the prisoners, especially those in the long central building. The warden made sure he was in plain sight when he topped up the glasses of his guests. A collective groan went through the whole gaol — a groan more felt than heard.

I went on to complete the last three weeks of my sentence without incident and at night I slept well, with the aid of a quiet nightcap. I was never short of smokes either. I was eventually discharged and got back to the station in time for mustering.

EVERYTHING IN THIS STORY has been made up from bits and pieces of stories from a number of prisons, and a number of blackfella ex-prisoners. These blackfella prisons did exist during a certain era of Australian history, in different places, at different times right across Australia. The prison in this yarn is a composite of all those old-time, blackfella gaols. And nobody can tell an entertaining yarn like a blackfella, ex-gaolbird, can tell it. The prison in this story does not exist. The town does not exist. Uncle Simon, Matron Dolly and Mr Middleton do not exist. Although, there were Uncle Simons and Matron Dollys in most of those old gaols.

Remember the gaolbird saying: 'Whatever happens inside these prison walls stays inside'? Well, this story was never written and this yarn was never told.

Glossary

You may have seen the word written Yammadgee, Yamadyi, Yamatji, Yammatji, Yamajee and so on; in fact someone once counted something like 28 variations.

The word written as Yamaji comes from the Wajarri language. Traditionally it was the word for an Aboriginal man from the Yamaji region, specifically a man who had reached a certain status. Today, in popular use, the word has come to mean any Aboriginal person from the Yamaji region. The Yamaji region encompasses, very roughly, the area starting from just north of Carnarvon, east to just past Meekatharra, south to around Paynes Find, then west to the coast.

Yamaji is now a generic term which includes people from the several language groups within the Yamaji region. (Note that the word never has an 's' on the end — Aboriginal languages don't use the English plural forms — so we can say 'many Yamaji attended the meeting').

The orthography, or writing system, of Wajarri was standardised and made official in 1992. This was when the spelling 'Yamaji' was confirmed. Before that, there was no standard system. People used to guess and put down their best effort.

The older spelling of 'Yamatji' was popularised mainly through the efforts of linguist Wilf Douglas, who worked in the Western Desert up to the 1980s. When he had a (from a distance) look at Wajarri and wrote it down, he used the Western Desert spelling system he knew.

Consequently some organisations had started using his 'Yamatji' spelling before agreement was reached on the Wajarri spelling of Yamaji. Other organisations which were formed later adopted the Wajarri spelling.
When pronouncing Yamaji, the stress is always on the first syllable, and the word is delivered phonetically.

Doreen Mackman (linguist)

A NOTE ON THE LANGUAGES USED IN THE STORIES

Indigenous people everywhere have always used three or four languages as a matter of course. In the same way, the author employs words from across the Murchison, Gascoyne and Pilbara regions, and in particular from Martu Wangka, a Western Desert and Wajarri, a Murchison language. These neighboring language groups often have words in common and, in some cases, these words may be spelt differently depending on the orthographic system used by the language group. Clarrie also uses colloquial terms and phrases from Aboriginal English.

WAJARRI WORDS

baja = angry, abusive, wild, savage

bardi = edible grub

bimba = edible gum obtained from certain trees

gami = grandparent, grandchild

giji = *Acacia pruinocarpa*, awattle with edible gum, its wood is used for making shields

gumbu = urine

gurarda = *Acacia tetragonophylla* or Kurara, a type of wattle

gurna = faeces

guwiyarl = *Varanus gouldii*, a type of goanna

mabarn = magic man, healer

mambu = shin, foreleg, knee

mardanyu = policeman

marlu = kangaroo (generic)

milyura = snake (generic)

ngaba = grandmother (nanna), grandchild

nyarlu = woman, female

thardunga = *Acacia craspedocarpa* or Hop Mulga. A type of shrubby tree with edible seeds from large, flat, wrinkled seed pods which contain many small green 'peas'.

winja = old person, grey-haired

wudaaji = 'little hairy people', small creatures like human beings believed by many Wajarri to have influence today

yalibirri = emu

Glossary

MARTU WANGKA LANGUAGE WORDS

kapi = water

kumpu = urine

jamu = grandfather, grandson

jurnpa = ash

kirriji = unmarried man

manjong = slow-minded,
  inexperienced

maparn = magic man, healer

marlurlu = initiate

marlu = kangaroo (generic)

mukuntu = lame, crippled, deaf,
  disabled

ngurlu = sacred area

turn-turnpa = promised girl

wayipa = used in greeting, (roughly)
  How are you? What's up?

wirla = gut feeling

**COLLOQUIAL LANGUAGE, STATION
ENGLISH AND ABORIGINAL ENGLISH**

bagging down = horse-breaking
  method where bags are rubbed over
  a horse to quieten it down

bareknuckle = fist fight

boomer = male kangaroo

dinner camp = occurs during
  mustering season where stockmen
  stop for a meal

dry wash = water course with no
  water

entire = stallion

hot curry = make trouble

lag = prision term for inmates serving
  a long sentence

lations = short for 'relations'

pannikin = big, tin cup

pink-eye = holiday from station work

plijiman = policeman

quart pots = stockman's small billycan
  that comes with a cup

sandy blight = eye infection, trachoma

skin = kinship term referring to a
  specific relationship between people
  in a language/cultural group

yellafella = Aboriginal person of
  mixed descent

About the Author

Clarrie Cameron is from the Nhanhagardi tribe of Champion Bay, Western Australia. Born into a strong family of Aboriginal rights activists, Clarrie attended Meekatharra Primary School then Carmel College, in Perth, working on pastoral stations in the holidays to pay for his education. He worked as a court officer for the Aboriginal Legal Service in the Pilbara. In 1972 he moved back to his grandfather's country in Geraldton to join the Department of Aboriginal Affairs. At the age of 50 Clarrie completed a Bachelor of Arts degree majoring in Aboriginal Affairs. Clarrie is a well-respected painter, carver and jewellery maker. He is also a committee member of the Yamaji Aboriginal Languages Corporation and the Yamatji Marlpa Aboriginal Council.